BLACKWOOD
1
VALLEY

GIN & GRUDGES

LAUREN PARKER RHODES

WILDFUL WRITINGS

NSW, Australia

www.laurenparkerrhodes.com; Instagram: @laurenparkerrhodes

Cover design: Okay Creations

Edited by Samantha | Radiant Editorial

ISBN (ebook): 978-1-7643071-0-9

ISBN (paperback): 978-1-7643071-1-6

Also by Lauren Parker Rhodes

Access Lauren's other books here, or at:
www.laurenparkerrhodes.com/books

DRIARN DUOLOGY
The Wife (short story prequel)
Amber Wolf
Blue Pointed Star

WHEN SECRETS BECKON

TRAITORS DUOLOGY
Traitors' Creed
Traitors' Promise

Author's note: Each of these books, with the exception of Traitors' Promise, were previously published by Lauren Searson-Patrick and have been republished, with permission, by Lauren Parker Rhodes. Traitors' Promise has only been published by Lauren Parker Rhodes.

AUTHOR'S NOTE AND CONTENT WARNINGS

You are about to embark on a small town romance. One I hope you enjoy immensely. There are, however, themes of childhood abuse and trauma one of the characters is still working through. These scenes are not graphic, but it is clear what the character experienced growing up. I have attempted to treat this subject with the sensitivity it deserves. If this is potentially triggering for you, please don't read Kade and Temperance's story.

Also, I am an Australian author, and you will find Australian English is the foundation of my books. As with everything, though, there is an exception! I cannot and will not use 'arse' over 'ass'. There is nothing sexy about 'arse' and (sorry!) there are no pirates in this story so 'ass' it is.

And a note to the reining and reined cow horse community: as you will know, the rules and structures of the different associations, how these sports do and don't cross association, state and international borders, can be quite variable. For ease and reading experience for everyone, including those not familiar with the reining/reined cow horse/ranch riding/camp drafting (and other) worlds in which there can be some crossover of skills, I have simplified the competition and registration structures. I hope you enjoy the little taste of reining in this primarily romance story!

For those of you who are a little bit (or a lot!) country at heart, love a cowboy or cowgirl in well cut jeans, and have impeccable taste in gin x

Chapter One

KADE

The room bristles around me. 'For fuck's sake, Kade, let it die,' my grandfather rumbles in his sandpaper voice. He slams the door behind him, leaving me standing in the living room, bridle still in hand, staring at the closed door.

'Let it die,' I murmur to myself.

If only I could.

But some dreams are hard to kill. And the dream of being able to ride one of the horses I train – in a headline competition – is not going anywhere.

I grip the worn leather straps crossing my palm. *Let it die.*

Exhaling a long breath, I try to do just that. My role on Wilder Station is as trainer and heir. Not that my grandfather values what I personally bring to either of those things. His knuckles have reminded me time after time – I'm not my father. My cheeks sting with the memory as I slowly spin on my heel, trying not to let my shoulders drop, and leave out the other door, the one that will take me back to the stables and round yard. Back to the horses that don't belong to me.

Back to the roles that don't feel like mine either. Trainer and heir sound good on paper, but the reality is, while my grandfather is in the picture, I will never have control over either.

The air is crisp this early in the morning, bitter as I suck it into my lungs. I'd worked myself up for months to ask him again – just one more time – to let me ride. The disappointment is metallic in the back of my throat, just like it was when I was a child. For a moment, the expansive blue, green, and brown farm around me goes black. All I can see is my grandfather standing over me. Spit flying from his mouth as he screams at me, his hand lifting—

Digging my nails into my palm, the one that holds the bridle, I count to ten as I walk the path to the stables by memory.

Ten as he fades around the edges; *nine* as his eyes dissolve; *eight* as his nose goes grainy; *seven* as the nausea in my gut starts to settle; *six* as I focus on my breathing; *five* as his mouth is all that's left of his face; *four* as the sound of my breath drowns out his words; *three* as the feeling of my cheekbone cracking starts to dissipate; *two* as the world around me begins to creep back in; *one* as his hand lowers and disappears into the sky as it begins to lighten.

For a breath I almost feel free.

But I'm still here. The same fences still surround me.

The memories that haunt me could be from a lifetime ago – they are, mostly. A lifetime most of this town doesn't know. Or at least doesn't talk about. There were plenty of people who, then, would have seen a little boy with purple surrounds to his eyes.

And so much black, purple, and then yellow, where they couldn't see.

Now, I know people see the image of my father when they look at me – a tall, broad man with a blond beard and piercing blue eyes. At least, that's what I remember of him from the photos my grandfather hid.

Clearing my throat and mind, I trudge down the dirt path to the tack room on the house end of the long run of stables. The old timber door looks fresh with the new sealant coat I gave it last weekend, and I shove it open. The bottom still catches a little – something I'll need to fix soon – and I place the bridle back on its hook, letting the door close after me as I walk back into the emerging sunshine. Hoping, like I do every day, that it could melt out all the memories that try to drown me.

'Hey,' Cami calls from the top of the round yard fencing. She's perched like a bird, before she sits, feet dropping to the next rung down. 'Going by the storm cloud of your face, I'm guessing he said "no"?'

I grunt at her, not something that makes me feel like a decent brother but, where Cami is concerned, the less she knows about the sort of person our grandfather really is, the better. She doesn't need to know she's the reason I stay. That I'll continue to stay long after she's left. I may not have – or have had – the ability to stop him when it came to hurting me, but I'd tear the skin from his body if he even *thought* about laying a hand on Cami.

And, whatever it costs me, I'll remain as heir to this station so I can ensure she gets her share. So she gets a shot at the life she deserves – one far away from Blackwood Valley and this township.

She towers over me as I reach her position on the top of the fence, folding my forearms on the top timber rail, and places a hand on my shoulder.

'Next time,' she says gently.

I don't tell her there won't be a next time. The fact I even need to ask for permission to compete on the animals I spend so many of my daylight hours training rubs against every fibre of my body. I hate that I still let that man control any of the things that are important to me. But somehow, looking him in the face always turns me into the little boy I once was. And maybe he's right, I'm not as young as I once was anyway. Maybe I'm better on the ground and not on horseback in a competition arena.

'When are you due at the bar?' she asks, a little note of hope in her voice. She's been bugging me to offer her a full-time job there for weeks now, and I will – when she's finished her study. When she's discovered how much more to this world there is than Blackwood Valley, and realised her teaching qualification could take her anywhere.

When she knows she's never coming back, and working with me for the rest of her life is the last thing she wants.

'*I'm* due at lunch, once I've given the horses a spin – we're only two months out from Nationals—'

'—and they won't work themselves,' she mimics, and I flick her thigh without uncrossing my arms.

She laughs as she half jumps, half slides off the shoulder-height fence.

'Fine, be like that. But you know I'm not going to stop asking until you say "yes".' She brushes the back of her jeans, lightness still in her voice. 'I'm bloody good for that bar and you know it.'

I mock-frown at her, stepping away from the fence. 'Finish your damn degree, and I'll think about it.'

She rolls her navy eyes, much darker than my own, and saunters in the direction of the house, heading back to the truck that's the same colour as her eyes. One that seems impossibly huge for her, but she manages it better than I do mine – not that I'd ever tell her that.

'See you tonight,' she calls across the flat space. 'I'm only three assessments away, oh brother of mine, so you'd better get ready – I have *plans*.'

I shake my head as I smile at her. Three? God, I thought it was still nine.

'I do have a business partner, you know,' I call after her.

'Oh please,' she shouts, stepping up onto the sidestep and hanging out the now-open driver's door. 'As if Jameson isn't going to be on board with new plans.'

Chapter Two

KADE

The bar Jameson and I own, Meadow and Velvet, is one street back from the main. Far enough away to not be found by every tourist that passes through, but close enough that those who bother to do any research can discover us. Our recent write-up in a national food and wine blog certainly didn't hurt our traffic.

The ribbed, tempered glass of the old saloon-style front doors is cool against my palm. I brush it gently before pushing on one of the matching, vertical brass plates and swinging one side open – it's become my silent hello to the place that's my safe haven.

'You're late,' Jamie says as I walk around the left side of the long, U-shaped bar, opposite the door I can hear swinging closed behind me.

'Had a sliding stop I had to nail on Pix,' I say. 'Just needed to get one good one in before his first reining competition and call it a day, and I did.'

'You don't get paid enough for the work you do on those horses. I'm pretty sure old man Carter paid me more as a farmhand. They must earn hugely in winnings, and you get, what? Two percent?'

I laugh. 'If that.'

Handing me money, even when I've earned it, is not my grandfather's style. I train the station's horses to keep our name strong in the industry, and in the knowledge that, one day, that station will belong to me and Cami.

I run a loving hand over the top of our smooth, shiny timber bar.

'No, this is the baby that keeps me fed,' I say with a smile.

'Yeah, well, she's going to be overrun tonight – we're sold out for the home gig of Juniper's tour.'

A spark of anticipation kicks in my gut. Between the blog and Juniper Hawthorne bringing her band here, we're going to get a lot of press. Good, customer-generating press that I'll gladly take. Even if it means Juniper's friends will likely be here as well – not that they've ever set foot in this place before. But if anything would force Temperance Archer to be a customer at Meadow and Velvet, it'll be Juniper playing here.

But having her – and her obvious hatred for me – in my own bar is ... disconcerting. I avoid her mostly, like I do with anything that associates me with my grandfather and his reputation, but that hasn't stopped her painting me with the same brush.

Jamie is grinning at me when I look at him, his dark skin almost gleaming in the subtle light of the bar. Handsome bastard. Sometimes I wonder if half our clientele is here for him. Jamie, his moustache, and my gin.

'We should have enough of the rosemary gin for the headline cocktail tonight,' I say, pressing myself back from the bar and taking in the brass shelves of every alcohol known to man. 'But let's add the sloe G&T to the board as another option.'

He sets the glass he's drying on the shelf behind him and picks up another. 'Max is coming tonight. She was asking after you yesterday.'

I groan; not this again. 'That's real nice of her, but no.'

'Kade, you need to start putting yourself out there. Time won't wait for you, mate. All you ever do is work.'

'And you're an expert on this, are you?'

Jameson has had his fair share of hookups from this very bar, but never anyone serious, despite how many might try to make it so. I could almost put him on the drinks board instead and take bids for his time.

His face falls, just a fraction. 'Yeah, I have an idea of how fast time goes. How quickly opportunities are lost.'

'Jamie.' I frown, a slight, uncomfortable pinch in my chest. 'Are you—'

The external door swings open, sunlight pouring in.

'Afternoon, boys,' Cami calls, her face completely hidden by a tower of boxes.

Jameson clears his throat and chucks his blue tea towel on the bench as he moves to help her. I stare at her, a little dumbfounded, as Jamie takes the top box so she can see where she's going.

'Ready to make this place sparkle?' she asks, giving me a challenging look.

'No,' Jamie and I say in unison.

'No sparkles,' I add, just to be sure she's clear.

There's a gentle thud as Jamie drops his box onto one of the dining tables at the opposite end of the bar. It always strikes me as a kind of magic how quiet it can be in here sometimes.

'Fine, fine,' Cami says, carefully lowering her boxes onto the same table and tightening her ponytail. Jamie eyes her warily. 'But tonight, we've got one of the biggest names in country music coming *here*. For an intimate, hometown concert. We want every person here tonight to feel like it's the best version of Blackwood Valley they've ever experienced, and leave everything else at the door. No stress, no worry, just the world's best gin and music to soothe the soul.'

Her voice is breezy, and I can't help but laugh as warmth floods me. Cami presses her palm to her chest and turns her face to the ceiling, as if she can hear and feel the music already.

Jamie just stares down at her, face unreadable.

'Alright, decorating fairy,' I say, walking towards them. 'Let's see it. But I'm serious about the sparkles.'

'No sparkles,' she confirms with a smile. 'This box' – she slides it to me along the table – 'can be unpacked on the bar.' She taps the top of another. 'This one can go on the stage. Jamie, you can help me get the last ones from the truck.'

He slides an indecipherable look at me before following Cami out the front door, and I can't help but turn and take in the hushed space.

What exactly does Cami think the best version of Blackwood Valley looks like?

Chapter Three

TEMPERANCE

Dusting the dirt from my knees, I stand – slowly, so my lower back doesn't gripe too much – and stretch my arms over my head for a moment. A smattering of dirt falls from my gardening gloves into my hair. The pile of weeds I've pulled from the garden bed is relatively small, which means I've been doing well at keeping up with them – so far, anyway. But if I'm right, and I'll have enough yield to keep up with the wedding season, weeding will remain a priority.

Nightshade huffs gently in the paddock on the other side of my young zinnias. The growing, coloured border runs along his fence line, but not so close he can stretch over and eat them – bad for him, and bad for my flowers. I watch him for a moment, aware he's noticing my every move even as he grazes quietly. He's the sort of horse my grandfather would have loved. Muscular without being too stocky. Athletic. Calm, with a centred disposition. And he can move. The trainer I'm paying knows he's good too – hence her eye-watering bills – and why these flowers are so important.

But there's only so much I can do with a horse like this now my grandfather is gone, and keeping him at competition standard is beyond my range. He's a dream to ride around the farm, something I often do to keep him humble, but I need Bree to ride him in the competition arenas.

I give the flower bud brushing my calf a little tap. *Any help you can give to his funds would be great.* If he wins, even at regional level, I might finally be able to invest back into Riverbow properly – the farm my grandfather loved so fiercely. I could fix up some of it and start seeing a better return. If we can get to Nationals, I'll get Riverbow Stud back on the map. That's what we need: qualifying scores in the three competitions – enough to get us to Nationals and get Nightshade on the country's radar as a stud stallion.

Nightshade's dark ears prick forward, away from me, and I turn to see a small, white car that looks entirely out of place coming down the long drive, the sound reaching me a moment later. I groan. Peeling my gloves off, I brace myself for discovery.

'Temperance!' Marlowe scolds as she steps out of the car, her gorgeous brown cowgirl boots sending up a tiny flurry of dirt as she slams the car door and walks to me. 'I knew I'd find you like this. You're not even showered!'

Marlowe, with her glossy dark locks straightened to perfection, and perfectly subtle makeup, has possibly never had dirt in her hair. I pull a face at her.

'Why did she have to choose there, of all places? Why *there*?'

Marlowe sighs, looking out over my farm as if it will give her patience, and not just an epic view down towards the river. She looks back to me with a resigned expression. 'I'm not doing this again. You know why she chose there – or her manager did – and you *will* be there to support her. Now get your ass in that shower before I hose you off out here.'

My chest pinches. Of course I want to support Juniper. Will and do support her. I just wish supporting her didn't mean supporting a Wilder at the same time.

'For fuck's sake,' I mutter. 'Give me twenty minutes.'

I spin on my heel and stalk towards the house.

'I'm timing you,' she calls, and I hear her following me to the side door.

'Five minutes left,' Marlowe says as I return to the kitchen, hair only half dry. 'Drink this.' She holds out a pale blue drink in a short glass.

'What is it?' I ask, before taking a full sip and closing my eyes. 'Oh, that's good.' I open my eyes and narrow them at her as I realise what I'm drinking – Kade fucking Wilder's gin.

'It's one of my favourites, and I knew you wouldn't order any tonight. You're welcome. Now hurry up and finish so we can go.'

I turn my back on her as I drain the delicious gin and tonic, letting the cool liquid slip luxuriously down my throat, then gently place the empty glass in the sink. Blowing out a long breath, I turn back to her, steeling myself to spend the night in a place I would normally never set foot – have never, and never intended to, set foot.

Until Juniper and her band blew up my plan.

'I've got a hip flask for you in the car,' Marlowe says with a frown. 'But I should warn you, it's not strictly legal to sneak your own alcohol into a licensed event.'

I can't help but laugh. 'Marlowe, you might just be the best lawyer friend a girl could have. And noted – I take the flask at my own risk.'

She's right, though. There's not a chance I'm spending a single dollar in a Wilder establishment, even if it does have great reviews in the same wedding magazines I've been researching for my flower business. Not after what they did my grandfather out of. Did me out of.

To my complete disgust, Meadow and Velvet is gorgeous. Oozing a sort of rustic, sophisticated charm with its long bar, timber floor, and the back-lit shelves of bottles lining the wall, intricate-looking glasses hanging beneath. In what looks like an eating area at the end of the space hangs a large photo of the river. My heart pinches. I love that view. And I know exactly where that photo was taken.

Asshole.

'This way,' Marlowe says, taking my elbow and tugging me to the left side of the bar, through the building noise and throng of people, underneath the greenery hanging from the high ceiling's rafters. I glance up at the lanterns dotted through the plants and almost feel like I've been whisked away to a magical world.

'We're here,' Marlowe declares, and I clear my throat as I take in the 'RESERVED: Marlowe' sign in the centre of our round table for three.

'Three?' I inquire, pulling a chair out, my back to the bar.

'Yeah, a friend from work was coming too, but she had to pull out – I promised I'd get her a souvenir. But Linden's going to join us later – once he gets Coco to bed and his mum can get there.'

I nod absently as I slide Marlowe's silver hip flask from my bag and pour the contents into my water glass. Marlowe's eyes are wide when I look up at her.

'What?' I ask. 'At least now I only have to do it one time. And let's be real, I'm going to need as much liquid assistance as possible tonight.'

Marlowe says nothing as she picks up the food menu, and I glance around the full bar. People are slowly filling the tables around us, their excited chatter warming my chest. The number here is tiny compared to the shows Juniper has played before, but these people – her hometown people – have looks of pride on their faces that I don't imagine I'll be lucky enough to see many times.

The hallway to the bathroom is to my right, and so far – I glance around again – there's no sign of any Wilders.

I allow myself a deep exhale and take a sip of the straight gin filling a little over half of my glass. *It's not as good as the one Marlowe gave me at the house.* Letting it run over my tongue, I reluctantly accept it will do. Could be nicer with a sprig of rosemary, though.

'I'll order,' Marlowe offers, pushing her chair back and heading to the bar. 'You're happy for me to choose, I assume?'

'Yes please,' I reply with a smile. Not only does she know I'm not going anywhere there could be direct interaction with a Wilder, but I always get food envy over whatever Marlowe's having, anyway.

When the food arrives, it confirms I was right to let Marlowe loose on the menu. Unfortunately.

'Why does it have to be so delicious?' I whisper.

She grins at me. 'Because, despite how hard you might wish it otherwise, food is not often tainted with ill feelings.' She tosses her head a little, flicking a piece of dark hair out of her face before picking up a deep-fried eggplant slider. It hovers halfway to her mouth when she pauses. 'Have you ever considered that it might be time to bury the hatchet? We both know it wasn't him that ...'

I stare at her as she trails off, letting the words *drugged your horses and got your grandfather disqualified before stealing the cottage* remain unsaid. Bury the hatchet? With the Wilders? Not a fucking chance. The only place I intend to bury a hatchet is deep in Kade Wilder's chest. His, or his grandfather's.

'No.'

⁕

Between the supporting band, the lantern lights, and my dwindling hip flask gin, Marlowe and I are a puddle of laughs by the time our plates are cleared. Even my cheeks feel warm as I press my fingers against them.

'Do you see a merchandise stand anywhere? I need to get a Juniper T-shirt or something,' Marlowe says, craning her neck to look around.

'No, but I need to visit the ladies, so I'll let you know what I find. Surely you could just ask Juniper for something, though?'

She purses her glossy pink lips. 'Maybe,' she muses, and I know it's not because she can't ask June. It's because she wants everything tonight to be about supporting June and buying official merchandise, as opposed to being gifted.

The women's bathroom is just as stunning as the rest of the building, with exposed stone walls and gold arched mirrors.

It makes me want to smash one.

Well, I don't actually want to bust up my knuckles – or break the mirror I'd love to have in my house – but it's still infuriating. Why does he get to be so successful after everything his family did, and I have to scrape by with next to nothing?

I run my fingers quickly through my dark auburn waves, trying to breathe some life into the air-dried mess of my hair, staring at myself in the mirror. *Not nothing*. I have the farm – dilapidated as some of it is – and Nightshade. And as a horse that can do both reining and cow work, he's got a really fucking good shot at winning in multiple competitions *and* being a sought-after stud horse.

I leave the bathroom and find myself in the dimly lit hallway once again. I can feel the beat of the music in my limbs and chest as I glance around – definitely no souvenir stand back here.

I pause. At the end of the hallway is a door clearly marked 'STOREROOM', and my heart beats a little faster than the bass. *What if I got my own souvenir?*

The door, painted the same dark, moody blue-grey as the rest of the hallway, doesn't make a sound as I push it open. Nothing but darkness greets me, and I slip inside, shutting the door behind me and gently groping the wall for a light switch.

I blink as the room illuminates – shit, even the storeroom is pretty. Open timber shelves with bottles and bottles of Wild Horse Gin, organised by colour, or perhaps infusion. The pendant light is made of rectangular glass panes in a brass surround and throws subtle shadows across the bottles. I smile. I am definitely taking one – maybe two – of them. Is that right? No. But the Wilders have no problem taking what doesn't belong to them, so why should I?

Chapter Four

TEMPERANCE

'A h ... hi?' a deep voice rumbles from behind me. I jump, turning back to the door.

To where Kade fucking Wilder now blocks my exit, his bright blue gaze narrowing as he takes me in. 'Wait – are you *stealing* from me?' he asks, disbelief dripping from his words.

Shit.

I slowly move the bottles behind my back, the weight of them straining my forearms thanks to the awkward angle. I thought I was being subtle, but the incredulous rise of his brows makes me wonder if that's true. My cheeks burn – but not as much as the fuzziness suddenly fogging my mind.

'No.' I scoff. Despite the fact that I am, in fact, stealing from him, the correct response still feels like 'no'. How much of that is the gin in my system, or the indignation of being caught, I don't need to examine.

'No?' he echoes, looking more than a little dumbfounded.

'No,' I repeat, refusing to acknowledge the awkward echo. Cursing myself for thinking this was a good idea, I step forward. Carefully drawing the two gin bottles from behind my back, I hold them out between us.

'I'm sampling,' I offer as I look up. 'Which would you suggest I start with?'

Belatedly, I realise I've stepped so close that the tops of the bottles brush the front of his checked navy shirt. I have to tip my head back to meet his gaze. My breath catches as the gold flecks in his blue eyes seem to glow.

'Sampling,' he murmurs, gaze narrowing again. Apparently he has the echoing problem too.

How can he seem to fill the room? It's small – little more than a large, very fancy cupboard – but it didn't feel quite so hot and airless before now. But that's the Wilder family, isn't it? Always sucking the life out of everything around them.

He stares at me and I hold his gaze, feeling like he could burn holes right through me with that look. But you don't back down from a Wilder. At least not at first. That's a lesson I have learned.

'Well,' he says slowly, shifting enough that the bottle tops press a fraction into his stomach. I watch as he takes the one from my right hand – the one with the pretty pale pink and gold label. His fingertips brush mine. 'This is one of my best gins. It's not on the sampling menu.'

He grips the bottle with firm, gentle fingers, and I swallow.

Juniper constantly tells me it's been too long since I was naked with a man. This weird, shimmying feeling under my skin tells me she's right – but there is no chance it's in response to *Kade*. It's just that his height and proximity, or the gin, or how freaking hot it is in here, have clearly addled my mind and body.

Kade reaches out to place the bottle back on the shelf before returning his attention to me.

'This one,' he explains, cupping the bottom of the bottle over my left hand without taking it from me, 'is the first run of the juniper and rosemary.'

His fingers drift towards the back of my wrist and a low throb unfurls between my legs. I stare at him, terrified he'll know how off-script my body has gone if I move. My heart thumps so hard I'm surprised he can't hear it. *It's just the touch*, I tell myself. I haven't been touched by someone other than Juniper or Marlowe in a long time. It's just the touch. Just the warm skin—

'It's simple but elegant,' he murmurs. His voice is low. Rough. And goosebumps break out along my arms.

I clear my throat. 'Sounds wonderful. I'm sure the girls will love it.'

He encircles the back of my wrist.

What the fuck is he doing?

And why don't I want him to stop?

'Not you? I thought you were *sampling*.'

His touch burns on my skin. 'I've changed my mind. I've probably done enough of that for tonight.' Probably. That hip flask of inferior gin is definitely what landed me here, in this storeroom, doing whatever the fuck this is with Kade. And now he's turning my body into a traitor.

So, yes, I probably should not have anything more, gorgeous-looking – and sounding – gin or not. But it's also exactly what I need right now. To get out of this room and get a drink.

'I'll get some tonic sent to your table,' he says, his hand dropping away before he slowly turns to the side.

I study him, my back almost against the shelves, his beard dipping towards his chest as he looks down at me. I try to keep calm as I brush past him and out of the storeroom.

With a bottle of not-so-stolen-gin in my hand.

'Oh, delicious,' Marlowe calls over the music as I return to our table. A flicker of worry crosses her face. 'Are we supposed to have a full bottle on this side of the bar?'

'No idea, but I was given it by someone who should know, so ...'

I smile at her, but I don't feel as victorious as I should. I was supposed to be taking a souvenir bottle of gin from Kade for myself. Not having him hand it to me while simultaneously making the world unsteady beneath my feet.

It takes two juniper and rosemary gin and tonics for my heart to stop racing. By the end of my third, Juniper is taking the stage and Marlowe and I are on the dance floor screaming the place down. The already dim lighting gets darker as June sits on her stool, guitar strap slung across her shoulder. She's radiant up there, and my eyes almost overflow with pride as she plucks the first few chords, the sound reverberating through my chest.

The crowd presses in as they begin to sway gently to her words, the bass guitarist sitting in a chair to her left watching every move she makes. Her voice and guitar are completely in sync with his.

'Drink?' a lady I don't know shouts next to me. I reflexively glance over my shoulder towards the bar, only to find Kade's eyes on me from where he's serving. A warm flush runs over me as I hold his gaze through the crowd, searching his; how is it possible he wasn't a complete asshole in that storeroom? How is it possible my body reacted in that way – a way it's still remembering?

My heart hammers as a man steps between us, catching my look, and smiles wide. He's got a nice, kind-looking face, but it doesn't make heat dance through my limbs like the memory of Kade's voice so close, so ... *enveloping* in that storeroom.

I must be way past drunk to be thinking like this. That's all it can be. Drunkenness and a dry spell. Two things I never should have brought to Meadow and Velvet. But it doesn't stop the flash of disappointment when the man, who is now making his way towards me through the mess of people, shifts enough for me to see the bar again.

Kade's gone.

Turning back to the stage, I let Juniper's song wash over me. The stranger next to me has seemingly forgotten her request for a drink and is dancing. *Neither of us probably needs more, anyway.* The thought drifts through me, hazy and soft.

Closing my eyes, I sway to the music. It's deep and sensual, and I can't help but let my body follow its rhythm. There is no one watching me here, and the darkness feels safe somehow. Maybe it's because all eyes are on Juniper, or because the magic she sings soaks into the air around me, but I revel in the loud, dark solitude, where I can let go – more than I have in a long time.

The person behind me presses a little tighter, and I let them into my space. The man with the kind smile appears in my mind, and I know I should turn around and say something, tell him I'm not interested. But – just for a moment – I let myself imagine it's a tall, unfairly broad blond man with a beard and short hair and eyes that glow a little in the low light. One that made me feel more alive in a short storeroom encounter than I have with any other man in a long time.

Fuck. A mini fantasy of a Wilder that didn't include murder. Maybe his gin isn't actually just gin.

I lift my hair off the back of my neck to let some air in. If it wasn't for Juniper performing here, I wouldn't have come. Giving business to the Wilders is not in my DNA. That driving instinct is obviously messing with me right now. Making me all scrambled. Making me want to know what it would like to be touched ... *more*, by someone like him. Well, someone who looks like him, anyway; even I can't deny he was graced by the good-looking-cowboy-gods. But I don't need someone with that last name anywhere near me.

Juniper starts her next song, her low, husky voice crooning to the audience, and the people in front of me leap excitedly, shoving me backwards. I stumble into the man behind me. He absorbs my movement by pressing his hard body against me, his hand finding my right hip.

I stiffen, readying to pull away.

'You okay?' Kade's voice washes down the side of my neck and over my shoulder.

His fingers tighten on my hip, and I can't breathe. The room seems to fade out of focus around me, the music thrumming through my middle.

'You decided to sample my gin after all.' His breath brushes my hair, and my scalp tingles before the shiver races down my neck.

'Maybe,' I say thickly, only half looking over my shoulder. 'Wasn't my favourite.'

'The number you had suggests otherwise.'

I huff a laugh. 'You have no idea how many I had. Perhaps I gave them all to Marlowe.'

His hand flexes. 'I watched you drink them, Temperance. I just wanted to hear you admit it.'

Oh, fuck. My name in his mouth is ... a lot.

Completely against my better judgement, I let myself relax against him, let his body press against mine. My back against his chest. My head against his shoulder. His hand slides around from my hip to my belly, and he holds me to him, fire pooling low in my gut, between my legs, as if it pours from his fingertips.

'I liked watching you drink my gin,' he murmurs against my ear.

Letting my eyes close again, I soak it in. Being touched – being held – by someone is enough to make my heart ache. It's not a feeling that belongs to me. And it's certainly not a feeling I should be borrowing from Kade Wilder. My head falls back as I count to ten. Ten beats to imagine what a different life could feel like. Ten beats to imagine what Kade could feel like. What would happen if his fingers slipped beneath my waistband.

I make myself step away. Fucking with the Wilders only ends in disaster for my family, and I will not be another moth to the flame.

'Give me your best next time, and perhaps I'll do it again.' I don't look at him as I shove my way through the crowd, back to the table, where I pour myself a glass of water.

I don't mean it, of course. There won't be a next time.

'Babe,' Marlowe says slowly as she arrives back at the table as well. The remainder of Kade's gin is gone, probably swiped by some opportunistic patron. At least I had the gumption to steal it from Kade directly. Sort of. 'Either that rosemary creation was way stronger than I thought, or I saw you snuggled up to the prince of your enemy on that dance floor.'

I shouldn't risk looking at her. She's a walking lie detector. But I can't help the instinct to look up, and I find her eyes narrowed on me with an unfamiliar intensity.

'It's really fucking strong,' I mutter. Surely that sums up what the hell happened.

'Text June and Linden that we'll catch them in the morning, and let her enjoy her adoring fans in peace. I need to sleep off the hangover I can feel coming.'

Chapter Five

KADE

I swirl the beer bottle by its neck. The weight of the liquid in the bottom pulls it into a small orbit between my knees where I sit in front of Jamie's fire pit. My palm still tingles with the memory of Temperance's soft stomach.

Fuck.

The rest of the night went perfectly. The band saw out the last three songs of their set, did their encore, and Juniper gave a heartfelt thanks to Jamie and me for hosting her, and to the town for turning up. Cleaning is never my favourite part of the evening but, between Jamie, Cami, and me, we got into a solid rhythm pretty quickly. The cleaning team will be in before opening to mop the floors and clean the bathrooms – really get rid of the night.

But all I could think about was Temperance Archer.

Her face when I busted her in my storeroom.

How she looked at me like she'd just discovered something. Something I've wondered about her a long time. From a distance.

The way she closed her moss-green eyes when she drank my gin.

How her entire body seemed to melt into mine, the swell of her ass against the top of my thighs.

Double fuck.

Temperance has always been beautiful, ever since we were kids. But even then I knew instinctively to stay away. Getting involved in any way with the Archers would incur a wrath from my grandfather the likes of which I could only imagine. The same way I knew not to tell anyone what it was really like to live with him.

I drown out the tremor that runs through me with a large pull of my beer.

'Easy.' Cami's voice comes from behind me. 'Wait for us – we're going to toast tonight.' Her laugh filters around my shoulders as she makes her way to the fire pit. The pit is full of fairy lights given it's fire season, and Cami takes a seat next to me, Jamie close behind and sitting on her other side.

She sighs loudly and contentedly as she sinks back into her camp chair. 'That was the best night *ever*!'

'Don't tell me you're fangirling over Juniper Hawthorne?' I ask, very aware of how close Juniper and Temperance are.

'Of course I am,' she replies. 'Why wouldn't I be? You saw her up there, heard her up there. She's incredible! And so nice.' She slides her attention to me. 'Did you see her friends were there too? Even Temperance Archer got herself into your bar to support her friend. Can you imagine having friends like that?'

'Cami, you do have friends like that – us,' I tell her, my chest uncomfortably tight. She's had a different experience of being a Wilder, and I hate the way she sees her lack of friends.

Jamie watches me carefully through the flickering light, but he doesn't disagree.

'Sure.' She waves me off. 'Having two *brothers* is great. But the friends weren't why the performance was so amazing.' Jamie drops his gaze; being an honorary Wilder isn't everyone's ideal, and he takes a sip of beer. 'Did you see people's faces when they walked in? We gave them an experience – a night of gentle magic. They felt good – happy.' She smiles. 'I loved it.'

I look between her and Jamie, the night air warm on my cheeks, Cami's radiance warming my chest.

We do make a pretty solid team, but I won't tell her how much until she finishes her teaching degree. I need her to have options outside my bar and the station. Not that our grandfather would give her a role there, even if I could find a way to make it safe for her. But when he's gone, it will be ours, and I'll make sure she has the freedom to contribute to the place our father loved.

Once she's lived a life outside this town.

'Well,' I say, sitting forward and holding out my beer bottle, 'cheers to making Cami happy.' I wink at her as our bottles clink together. I stretch out to catch Jamie's. 'And cheers to the impeccable job she did pulling off the final touches for tonight.'

'To making Cami happy.' Jamie clears his throat. 'And the three of us killing it tonight.'

Cami giggles and tips her head up to the night sky, sinking back again in her chair. 'We *have* to do that again,' she insists, and I shake my head with a smile. 'There are so many acts we could bring in, events we could host. Meadow and Velvet is the best gin bar in the whole valley, and several regions beyond. We can take it even further.'

Her excitement for the business Jamie and I built is almost intoxicating. It's probably not surprising, given she's been watching and cheering us on since the very beginning – right when I started making my own gin and she drew me design after design for the labels.

'Graduate. Get a job. Leave town. After that,' I tell her for the millionth time, 'we'll chat. But, for now, I'm out.' I drain the rest of my drink and stand. 'Cami, crash here, okay?'

'Sure, why not?' Jamie says. 'Your brother does.'

'You love having us here,' I point out.

He groans. 'I do, it's true. But shit, Kade, I wish you'd just move in properly and stop living out of that fucking bag in there. Set yourself up. That station is not your home, mate.'

'Night,' I murmur, completely ignoring his statement.

My grandfather's farm might not be my home in the way he means, that's true – I don't have one of those, except maybe Meadow and Velvet. Or the abandoned cottage on the south border of the station – the one I dream of sometimes. But the station will be my home one day, and giving up any stake in it now would be a mistake. And my horses are there – I might not be able to get a name for myself riding those ones, but everyone knows I train them, and that's just as important.

I need it to be.

Pix easily did the best in the warm-ups I took her and the others through this morning. Now, watching Brody Smithdon – who won the National Title the last two years running – ride her, she seems almost light years ahead. She's not, and there's always a lot that can go wrong in a competition arena, but when you're dealing with some of the best horses in the state – and, hopefully, the country – the small things separating them make a world of difference.

Tray Headon, a rider whose wins aren't as impressive as Brody's on paper, but who has the potential, is on my chestnut gelding. There's some finessing they can each do, and the steady look of concentration on Tray's face tells me he's focused on slowing it down, regulating his breathing, and working with the horse, not against him.

The faint sound of footfalls behind me stiffens my spine. My grandfather stands next to me, and the way I suppress my flinch is so practised it's second nature. He's almost as tall as me – I nudged taller than him in my mid-twenties – and still strong. Still proud.

'They're looking good,' he says – the words positive, the tone disapproving.

I make a sound of agreement. I don't have the energy for much more with him. Not only am I tired after last night and an early morning, the rejection of riding in the competition still stings.

He laughs. 'Still sore, are you?'

I frown. 'Of course not. I just don't understand it – I ride at least as well as Tray,' I say quietly. 'And it would look good to have a Wilder win on a Wilder horse.'

He turns to me, his gaze heavy as he studies my profile.

'Lookin' good has never been my priority, son,' he says. 'Being the best is what's important on this station. We hold our place as the largest, most profitable, most powerful station in all the states this side of the country, and have done for decades now. That is not a position I will cede because you want to get a ribbon on your fucking pony.'

The jab lands, as he knew it would. But what he doesn't know is that my riding isn't as good as Tray's – it's better. And I'd give Brody a run for his fucking money too.

But instead of winning championships, I'm subsumed into the 'trained by Wilder Station' on the entry forms. Not even my name is listed.

'And just so we're clear,' he adds, 'if you even *think* about riding someone else's horse, you'll lose all access to my horses.'

I fight the urge to hang my head. We both know there's no one in this state – and likely others – who would cross my grandfather by letting me ride without his endorsement. All the same, it's another option he's taking away.

As I watch the horses I trained impeccably go around the arena without me, for a moment I'm jealous of Temperance. Because while I have to hide and cower and obey, she can hate my grandfather right out in the open.

My fingers tingle at the memory of her stomach beneath my hand, at the phantom pressure that won't leave me alone.

It's the thought of her hatred that makes me push her from my mind. She deserves to be as far from my grandfather as possible.

Chapter Six

TEMPERANCE

Blackwood Valley's night markets are something to behold. With the large park in the centre of town lit by fairy lights, and gentle spotlights that illuminate the tree trunks, it's already magical. Add in the different stall-holders, the live music, and the best food from around the region, and it's one of my favourite places to be.

It's grown substantially since I was a child but, even then, it was one of my most loved things to do in the summer. Now I get to enjoy it as an observer rather than a participant, as I set up my flower wagon and sell a variety of arrangements to locals and tourists alike.

I rarely have the same things available; what I can bring depends on how the season has gone and what I keep aside for weddings. It's something that started out of necessity, but now seems to be a drawcard for people to buy as much as I have available on the night.

'Peri,' a little voice calls from under the wagon. My heart warms at the use of my schoolyard nickname, something half the town still calls me now, but something that started with my closest friends. 'Did you know how much dirt comes down here?'

I laugh. 'Yeah, Coco, that's kind of a hazard of growing things in the dirt – it sticks.'

I crouch and poke my head under the wagon to find Linden's niece on her back in the grass.

'What are you doing under there?' I ask. 'I thought you were my helper today?'

'I'm just taking my break.'

Her voice is serious and I have to bite back a smile. I think she 'worked' for about ten minutes. But while I really do love spending time with her, it's Linden I'm keen to give a break. The loss of his sister, Bridie, hit our town hard. Unsurprisingly, despite his overwhelming grief, Linden stepped up to raise Coco.

Coco turns her head to me, the green grass contrasting with her night-dark hair. 'Do you think there could be ghosts under here?'

I pull a face. 'Well, I certainly hope not.'

'It could be cool.'

'Ghosts might make my gin change colour.'

I jump at Kade's voice, smacking my head on the underside of the wagon and cursing.

'Kade!' Coco squeals, scrambling out and leaving me rubbing the back of my head as I stand.

I watch, scowling, as she runs to him and starts peppering him with questions about his horses. With one hand on her shoulder, he waves to the truck idling nearby. It slowly backs up, my palms starting to sweat as it dawns on me what he's doing.

'You're not here,' I protest, brushing down the front of my dress. 'We are not neighbours.'

He looks sideways at me. Likely because we are, in fact, neighbours. His blue gaze pins me, just like it did the other night, and the sounds of the other stallholders preparing go fuzzy around me. I give my head a little shake – I did hit it pretty hard – and look away.

'I got an email this morning. Our location changed, and we're here tonight,' he explains quietly. 'I double-checked.'

Fuck.

Unfortunately, he's probably right. The little I know of Kade hasn't given me reason to doubt he's organised. And surely after the absolutely-out-of-character craziness from both of us at Juniper's concert, he'd be as keen as me to keep his distance.

I take a step away. 'Right. Coco,' I call, holding my hand out to her, 'you're not old enough to be behind there, sweets. Let's get the rest of these flowers on show.'

As whoever it is – Jameson, probably – backs the truck up to Kade's gin stand site, he gently guides Coco back to me. I try to focus on Coco and how her nose scrunches when she smiles, but it's impossible not to follow the line of Kade's arm up to his shoulders and the breadth of his chest in the white T-shirt he's wearing.

My breath catches as he takes the last step into my stall space, then another, and another, until he's right beside me. Until all I can smell is Kade mixed with my flowers, and I think my vision might start spinning.

'How's your head?' he asks gently, drawing my gaze from his chest to his face. To where his lips are almost hidden in his beard.

Stupidly, I cup the back of my head as if checking it's still there. But there's nothing more than a dull ache to show for the impact. I don't know what's thrown me more – that I hit it, that Kade is my neighbour tonight, or that he genuinely seems to care.

I don't respond, and something in his expression shifts as he searches mine. 'Well, I have painkillers if you need them,' he says, before leaving Coco with me and moving to unpack his truck.

As the sun begins to set, washing the Blackwood Valley township in colour, people start to arrive at the market. The balmy summer evening is like a magic in itself, soaking all the market-goers in golden warmth. My cheeks hurt from smiling as I talk to everyone who stops by, studiously trying to ignore the fact that I feel Kade looking at me far more frequently than he should.

'It's so lovely to see locally grown flowers,' Doris remarks, taking the bunch she just purchased. 'You do them so well. I'd love to stock some in the bakery if you have enough?'

My stomach flutters. 'Oh, that would be—'

'They'll look beautiful next to the little shelf of Wild Horse Gin,' she adds, likely with no idea how much that pisses me off. 'Speaking of, I'm headed there next.'

I force a smile as she takes the three steps to the tall stand where Kade and Jameson are selling their gin and giving free tastings.

Kade catches my eye, throwing me an indecipherable look before turning his full attention to Doris and leaving me feeling a little colder for it. Jameson laughs easily at something his customer says, and then his focus becomes completely absorbed by something through the throng of people. I glance over but can't tell what he's looking at, other than Camilla Wilder making her way through the crowd. But when I steal another look at Jameson, he's back to laughing with his customer.

'How much is the white bouquet?' a voice cuts in. I mentally shake myself. Studying Kade and his friends isn't going to get me anywhere.

'Thirty dollars,' Coco replies, and I nod at her. 'If you want ribbon, it's forty-five.'

The man before us gives me a wide-eyed look, and I can't help but laugh.

'She's a good sales assistant,' I tell him. 'But there's no extra charge for ribbon.'

Coco elbows me in the hip. 'Don't say that,' she whispers harshly. 'Kade says people should always pay what's right for what they want.'

I almost choke as I hand the man his change and flowers. If only Kade wasn't a child when it came to paying my grandfather his share of the winnings *before* his own drugged our horses.

'Evening, folks.' A deep male voice cuts across the park from the loudspeakers; my skin crawls. 'I'm Walter Wilder,

Chair of the Blackwood Valley Council, and it's an honour to welcome you all here tonight.'

Despite everything in me screaming not to, I slide my gaze to Kade.

As Kade's grandfather drones on about our town, how much we value tourists, and how we welcome them to our different events – all things I'd agree with if someone else was saying them – I can't help but wonder why Kade seems as uncomfortable listening to him as I do.

At the same time, it's a good reminder. Whatever complete lapse in judgement I had in Meadow and Velvet, I *will* be keeping my distance from both Wilder men.

'Hi, Kade.' I hear Maxine's sultry tones as soon as Walter's voice gives way to the night. She slips onto the barstool closest to my end of Kade's stall and crosses her legs. 'What have you got for me tonight?'

Kade clears his throat, and I roll my eyes. They'd make a sickeningly good-looking couple. I know they're not together; there's no way Maxine – our local and somewhat celebrity wedding planner – could keep that to herself. But I'm pretty sure she wouldn't turn him down, and that thought has me feeling snarkier than it has any right to, especially because I owe so much of my flower business success to her.

'I'm dreaming up some new stuff,' Kade says, 'so most of this you've already tried. But I do have one of the last of the navy strength, if you want one of those?'

Maxine gives a throaty laugh and tosses her hair a little. 'You know I love it strong.'

Jameson coughs, but it's Camilla's gaze I meet when I glance up. Looking away quickly, I try not to notice how Maxine is leaning forward over the temporary bar, or how she circles one red-painted fingernail around the rim of her glass. And I certainly try not to notice how Kade fills out his shirt and pours with precision as he smiles at her.

No. I look at the diminishing bundles of colour on my wagon, and at little Coco laughing with our next customer, who asked – I think – if our sunflowers really hold the sun. This is where my attention belongs. Maxine and Kade can do whatever they like. Provided I don't hear Walter's voice anywhere but in these public forums, I'm good.

Chapter Seven

TEMPERANCE

B ree is late.

Nightshade is saddled, I've warmed him up, and now I'm standing next to a post, his reins tied securely, thirty minutes after Bree was supposed to be here. If she's not here in ten minutes, I'm going to have to unsaddle him and put him back in the paddock before I get myself to work.

And we'll be no closer to winning that competition.

My phone buzzes in my pocket, and I almost drop it in my haste to answer – Bree.

'Hey,' I say, 'you okay?'

'Well ... define "okay"?' She sounds like she's on the other side of the world, and my forehead starts to prickle with sweat.

'What's happened, Bree?'

She half laughs, half sobs. 'I came off—'

My heart sinks into the depths of my stomach. 'How bad?'

'Snapped radius and concussion.' She sniffs. 'I'm just leaving the hospital. But I'm out, Peri, I'm sorry. I can't ride him.'

I drop my head to the worn timber railing of the round yard fence and let the scratchy surface dig into my skin.

'Are you okay, though?' I ask, hoping the rising panic in my throat isn't colouring my words.

'I will be, I guess. He was – he was going to be my shot, Peri. And I'm out. I—'

Nightshade nibbles my hair. He was my shot too. I push down my rising nausea, thinking of the debt I need to pay. The ute I need to fix. The horse feed I need to buy.

Shit. Some would tell me that having so much hinging on one horse winning a few competitions is reckless. Madness. But they don't understand this business. This isn't a ride for fun; this is about my livelihood.

'It's okay, Bree,' I hear myself say through the pounding in my ears. 'There'll be another show. He has time. Next year will be ours – I know it.' I hope it doesn't sound as much of a lie to Bree as it does to me. Nightshade will be able to compete for a few years yet, but I won't be able to afford to keep him that long without a win. Not in competition shape. 'Can Ryan get time off to look after you?'

'Yeah,' she replies, the cracking in her voice gaining momentum. 'He's here.'

'Good, that's good. I'm going to come see you soon, okay? You just rest up, let that boyfriend of yours take care of you, and focus on getting better so we can win this thing next year. We can do it, Bree, I know we can.'

She cries a bit harder before saying goodbye and hanging up.

Nightshade huffs against my cheek, and I slowly stroke his soft dark nose, the world feeling like it's falling away beneath me.

My best shot at being able to restore my grandfather's farm, make it comfortable enough to live on, and re-establish his stud, just fell off a fucking horse.

Flowers. For the next six to eight hours of my life I need to focus on them, and not the free fall I've been trying to hold my mind back from since Bree's call. Set in one of the state's most picturesque valleys, less than an hour from the closest major city, Blackwood Valley has no lack of people coming for events. Weddings, mostly, but people flock here for everything from babymoons, to corporate getaways, to the different community gatherings that celebrate the turning of the seasons and all that goes with it.

And what does every good, picturesque small-town event need? Flowers. A product I have been working my ass off to become a supplier for.

'They're going to want white and yellow for their summer wedding,' Maxine says as we stand in line for coffee. 'I can tell. Can you work with that?'

I nod, thinking of the baby's breath already on its way, and the yellow dahlias that should flower in the next couple of months. I wonder if they'd prefer dahlias or billy buttons?

'The Anderson's' order will be ready for next week too,' I reply as we step forward, trying to let our business chat distract me from the memory of her batting her lashes at Kade at the night market.

In the warmer months our meetings are almost weekly, and Maxine and I have perfected the art of business over coffee. We sit and look at photos – often the bride's wedding mood board or the venue – and then finish off before grabbing a takeaway coffee to fuel us through the rest of the day. At times, I see her more than I see my best friends, and I have nothing but admiration for how she's built her business; I've learned a lot from her. All the same, the way she leaned into Kade at the market doesn't feel like something I want to see again.

'Excellent. If you drop it at town hall by 10 am, I'll have one of my assistants do the arrangements so you can get to your horse thing.'

My chest feels sluggish as I sigh.

'That's not going to matter anymore,' I say with a sigh, stepping forward again as the line continues to grow behind us. 'Bree came off – she's out.'

Maxine whips her head to me, her dark-brown, chin-length hair flying outwards in the process. 'Shit, is she okay? Are you okay? You'll find another rider, right?'

I shake my head, willing the tears away. 'Honestly, I don't know that I can. Bree was so good with him – they were working together almost seamlessly – and I'm just not sure she's replaceable. Stallions can be ... particular. Plus, even if someone good enough was free, I'd never be able to afford them.'

'You have to pay for someone to ride him?'

'Normally, yeah. Bree's so young, riding Nightshade was going to give her some great experience as well. Everyone else out there has the price tag that matches their experience.'

I don't tell her that even Bree's fee was a huge stretch for me and Riverbow Ranch.

'You can't do it?' Maxine asks with a concerned look as we reach the top of the coffee pick-up queue.

I bark a laugh. 'I can ride, but I can't *ride*. Once upon a time, we bred to sell to riders and trainers and then ...' I wave my hand to indicate all the things that went down with Walter Wilder. Things most of this town know enough about to understand it wasn't a great time for us. Not that they helped in any real way. It was my grandfather who took the fall for Walter's abuse of their shared horse. 'Well, things got harder, and then Grandad got sick, and there was no coming back from there. Nightshade was supposed to be my way of getting the stud back on the radar. Show the reining world what our *bloodlines* can do, not what I can do as a rider.'

My paper coffee cup is warm as I pick it up, and I all but hug it.

'Shit,' Maxine says, turning to me with her own coffee in hand. I study the way her deep-red polished nails contrast with the black paper cup. 'I'm really sorry, Peri. If there's anything I can do ...'

'Like get in the saddle?' I ask, looking back up at her face.

It's her turn to laugh. 'Not in a million fucking years. See you Friday?'

'Friday,' I agree, desperately hoping I won't be begging her for a wedding-planning assistant job in the near future. In a few short months, my income will get tighter as the season starts to fade.

'Right,' Maxine says, buttoning her cropped blazer with one hand. 'I've got the Youngs for a wedding venue tour in twenty minutes, and I'll be in touch when I know more about what their floral choices are.'

'Good luck,' I call after her as she swings her bag over her shoulder and heads for the door onto Main Street.

As I turn to follow her out and return to my flowers, I almost run straight into the person behind me.

Camilla Wilder gives me a tentative smile that tells me she heard everything, and my stomach turns to acid. The last people in this town I need knowing any of my business – least of all my horse business – is the Wilders.

Chapter Eight

KADE

'Absolutely not.'

I can't help but gape at Cami. Has she gone fucking insane? Me? Offer to ride for *Temperance Archer*?

I laugh.

'Honestly, Cami, I—' I shake my head at where she sits on the other side of the bar, my hand frozen mid-wipe. The cloth is lukewarm and wet in my palm.

'Kade,' she insists, leaning into the wooden edge. 'Think about it. Grandfather has said "no". You are *never* going to change that asshole's mind. He likes controlling you, he always has and—'

'Cami.' I will patience into my voice, trying not to wince at the idea of my grandfather knowing about this conversation. 'Not only would he throw a fit so epic we'd be homeless – literally – there is no way in the world Temperance Archer would agree to me, a Wilder, riding her prized stallion. Seriously, how can you be entertaining this right now? And what about the horses I already have responsibility for? What happens to them if he strips my access?'

I don't know all the details of what went down with Gabe Archer, Temperance's grandfather, but I'm confident he wasn't alone in the drugging scandal, even if he was the one disqualified from ever competing again.

'How?' she asks immediately, zeroing in on that question, and I know she's not expecting an answer. No, I'm about to get a Camilla Wilder special.

'Because,' she says, 'this is your dream, Kade. I know you don't need me to remind you of that. It's your fucking *dream* to be a competitive rider, and I'm delivering that dream to you. Blackwood Valley's best stallion is suddenly riderless – he's trained, he's registered in the next three shows, and all you need to do is qualify in each of those and you'll go to the big one.'

She takes a single breath before continuing. 'As for the others, he won't let any harm come to them – they're worth too much money.'

And he doesn't have a scapegoat.

The idea of riding in the region's largest reining competition on the Archers' Nightshade is a thought that has hooks. Hooks that sink fast and deep.

But there's not a chance Temperance would say 'yes'. She would have said 'no' any day, but after the night here at the bar – when I found her in my storeroom and held her on the dance floor – the answer will be a 'fuck, no'. Heat seeps into my limbs at the memory, and I grip the now-cold cloth tighter. Whatever lapse that was, I'm absolutely sure the woman who literally crosses the street to avoid me will not agree to this.

'Kade! Are you listening to me?' Cami waves a hand in front of my face. 'She's going to bow out. She has no other options right now. Do you really think she's not desperate enough to let you ride?'

'Thanks,' I grumble.

'Come on, Kade, you're a damn good option, and you know it. You ride a top-tier horse that's not owned by the man pulling your strings and prove yourself on your own merits – she gets her stallion noticed, and maybe her stud starts to find its feet.'

I give up all pretense of cleaning and fold my arms across my chest. If I have a hand in getting an Archer business off the ground, Grandfather will be spitting mad. Even more so than when I suggested I could invite the pretty girl from school – Temperance Archer – to my ninth birthday party.

The Archers were our friends, then our competition, and now they are nothing, he'd screamed. *We do not associate with vermin.*

The memory is sharp, but I push it away; sharp memories and talking about the man who raised me go hand in hand. But when I went back to school the next day, pain radiating down my legs with every step, I still thought Temperance was the prettiest girl I'd ever seen.

And not once have I thought of her differently, even after all this time.

I shake my head to dislodge the idea that I could ride that stallion. *Her* stallion. 'Hypothetically ... if we were even going to attempt this,' I say slowly, and Cami's face lights up. 'And I'm not saying I will. But *if* we were to find a way for Temperance to even consider this crazy idea, you can't be there. You can't live at that station with him if I'm in any way involved with an Archer.'

She nods solemnly, her blonde ponytail bobbing. 'Yeah,' she breathes, 'I know.'

'Is there anyone—' I start, but she shoots me a withering look. My chest falls. Cami and her worry about friends. 'I'll pay for you to stay at the bed and breakfast by the river while you're still on university break.'

'What about you?' she counters.

I look around the closed bar. 'Jamie will probably—'

'What?' he asks, as he pushes through the swing doors to the kitchen and joins me behind the bar.

'You'd have Kade stay at your place for a while, right?'

Jamie looks between us, his gaze lingering on Cami a little longer than me and, not for the first time, I breathe a little easier knowing I'm not the only one who looks out for her. I don't have to tell Jamie what living with my grandfather is like – he's known me long enough, through enough avoided high school gym change rooms, to have worked it out.

'As long as you both need,' he answers, raising a brow. 'Not that it'll seem much different to normal. Haven't you basically lived with me on and off since we were sixteen?'

I scoff a laugh. He's not wrong – I'm there more than I am in what's supposed to be my wing of the station. At one point, I desperately wanted Jamie to live at the huge station with me, but subjecting him to my grandfather wasn't something I was prepared to risk.

'That's cool, man,' I say. 'I'll put Cami up at Lamona's.'

He frowns. 'Why?' He shakes his head. 'It's so ... isolated out there.' Worry flickers over his features as his dark brows lower.

Cami shifts on her barstool. 'It's fine,' she murmurs, looking at me. 'That'll suit me.'

I run my dry hand through my short beard, thinking it over. Lamona's is down by the river – not quite at my favourite bend, the one in the photo on the wall, but far enough out of town on the road to Whimsy Ridge. More importantly, it's somewhere my grandfather wouldn't think to look for her. Not that I expect he will; he's never given two shits about my baby sister, for no reason other than she's a woman. Even when I wasn't enough to absorb his rage, he didn't turn his fists – or his belt – on her, and I'll forever be grateful for that. Even if it makes the familiar twist of my anger burn in my chest.

He is so undeserving of her. He didn't touch her, but he's left his toxic mark all the same.

'Cami,' I say, chucking the now-drying cloth into the sink, 'is it too far? Do you want to stay with Jamie and me?'

'No,' she replies quickly, just as Jamie adds, 'Please.'

She glances at him, cheeks turning pink, probably hating the attention. 'I'm a big girl,' she points out, turning back to me. 'The B&B is fine. Good. It's not like it's forever, anyway. I've got to go back to uni for my last assessments.'

Staring at the timber bar top, the possibilities – and the risks – swirl through my mind.

'So you'll do it?' she presses after a moment, the only other sound Jamie stacking clean glasses onto the shelves behind us.

I sigh. I can't say I'm not tempted by that stallion. But just as tempting is the thought of having a reason to be closer to Temperance. Is that madness? My grandfather ruined hers. The Wilders are single-handedly the reason her grandfather died with nothing but the run-down farm she's trying to rebuild. It's why she avoids me at all costs, but if I were her, I'd shoot me on sight.

The way she softened against me *after* she heard my voice plays on repeat. My heart hammers, and I turn away from Cami before my jeans get uncomfortably tight.

Taking a deep breath and focusing on how the inhale stretches the fabric of my T-shirt, I turn back and lean against the bar. I could *ride*. Really fucking ride.

But there's a very good chance my grandfather will do worse than just take my horses.

My shoulders drop as the thought sinks in. 'Cami, no.' I shake my head. 'I can't – we need that station. I can't risk it.'

The bar goes quiet as the three of us look between each other.

'Maybe it's time to call his bluff,' Jamie says. He turns slowly as we both stare at him, resting a hand on the bench behind the bar. 'Cami's right – the horses you train will be fine. You've done what you can for them. See how he copes without you.'

I blink at him, heat prickling the back of my neck. *Call his bluff?* Could it be that simple? No. I know better. At the same time ... there's no way Temperance will say yes anyway. What would it cost to ask her? Maybe my pride at the rejection, but how can that be worse than being turned down by him every damn time?

'Do you have a plan on how to tackle the approach?' I inquire.

Cami squeals and claps, and a smile spreads across Jamie's face as he wipes his hands on the tea towel tucked into his front pocket.

'You're friends with Marlowe, right?' Cami asks him.

Chapter Nine

TEMPERANCE

The smell of Doris's bakery is like inhaling a bathtub of joy. A croissant-scented, warm one that I never want to leave. It's as busy as I expect this morning, and exactly why I chose this time to drop off the flowers she sells for me.

Her shop is long and narrow, with domed glass displays running almost the full length of one wall. The opposite side is lined with old timber shelves dotted with local goods and produce, including a display of Wild Horse Gin. I frown. I knew it would be here, but the colours of both the bottles and their beautiful labels complement my flowers *far* too well.

'Peri, my darling!' Doris calls from behind the counter, over the heads of several people in front of me. 'Oh,' she gasps as she reaches me, spying the flowers in the tubs at my feet. 'I love them. Let's get them out. How're your mum and dad?'

Smiling, I hand her a vase full of my favourite – vibrant pink cosmos. 'Good. They're loving being at Lake Wildes. It's different to our valley township, of course, but I think the lifestyle suits them after so many years on the farm.'

She nods, brushing her hands down her apron before taking another jar from my tub. I watch her place it on the shelf. 'Yes,' she says quietly. 'There were some hard years there for them. But it's wonderful to see you breathing new life into that place.' Doris turns back, hands out for the next jar, and I pass her one dotted with lavender. 'I fear the other side of that equation has a bit further to go, but he's come so far. It's not easy to step outside the shadows of our forefathers. Especially when his parents are no longer able to show him the way.'

I pause, knowing she's talking about the Wilders. Kade in particular. No matter how far I try to distance myself, it always comes back to our two families – the Archers and the Wilders. And as much as her words circle in my mind, I can tell she's also thinking about her own history.

But the mention of Kade's parents chips painfully at me. Despite everything between our grandparents and the havoc Walter Wilder wrought on our home, I grew up with two loving parents, people who still support me and my businesses even though they no longer live in town. Kade and Camilla, on the other hand, lost their parents so young I sometimes wonder if they even remember them.

Doris chatters on as we work in the tight space between the queue and her shelves, the gentle din around us muffling half her words. But her smile is warm, and her support even warmer.

The old tins I chose for my miniature bouquets look right at home, and I adjust one of the ribbons. The larger bouquets are tucked into an assortment of recycled vases and vessels I've sourced over time.

'Well,' Doris remarks, stepping back with a smile, 'I think that'll do it. I'm not even sure they'll last the morning!'

As I move back to admire our work, I bump into someone behind me.

'Oh, I'm so—'

Kade cocks his head, a smile tugging at his mouth under the beard. 'Hi there.'

'Kade, how lovely,' Doris says, squeezing in beside me. We all stand far too close as the bakery bustles on. 'I was just talking about you.' She ducks to the crate at his feet while Kade gives me a quizzical look, my cheeks heating. 'Ah, yes. I do love this one.' She stands without shelving the bottle. 'Might keep it for myself.' She winks, then peers at the growing queue. 'Righto, I better help this lot. Peri, you'll help Kade with the gin?'

I swallow, the weight of Kade's gaze pressing into my cheek. 'Of course, Doris,' I murmur, hoping she doesn't notice the tightness in my voice.

'Want to tell me what you were saying about me, or shall we unpack?' Kade asks quietly, nudging the crate closer with his boot as he makes space for the line behind him.

My stomach shimmies at the low timbre of his voice – or perhaps it's the hint of mirth – and I scramble for a retort.

Someone claps him on the shoulder and he returns the greeting before turning his attention back to me. His focus is so intense it feels like one of Doris's decadent desserts. I tighten my ponytail, and his gaze tracks the movement.

'Let's just get this done,' I mutter with a sigh.

We work side by side. His arm brushes mine each time he reaches for the crate, passing me a bottle to shelve. The accidental contact makes it impossible to forget that night at his bar. The night he—

No. I will *not* let my mind go there. I'd sooner take Juniper's advice about trying one of those bloody dating apps – which I'm not keen on either. But I definitely don't want to fall into whatever warm, soft-edged fondness Doris clearly feels for him.

Almost instinctively, I group the bottles with flowers and other items in matching colours – a bakery-style colour block.

I love it.

When I look up, Kade's smile is wide, his arms crossed over his pale blue T-shirt.

'Looks good, Temperance.'

I clear my throat. That stupid smile is so at odds with everything I expect from his family. His horse-drugging, lying grandfather would never smile like that.

'Excellent. Happy to be of service,' I snap, grabbing my tubs and heading for the door, acutely aware he's following.

Outside, the noise lessens, the chatter of those lucky enough to get one of the few outdoor tables drifting on the summer breeze.

'Peri,' Maxine calls as she strides towards us. 'You better have enough flowers for my weddings – Kade.' She smiles as he steps out behind me.

She looks between us and purses her lips. The sound she makes is far too amused. I glare.

'Max,' Kade says, his voice nothing like the one that ran down my skin that night. Then, it was warm and enveloping. Now, it's polite. Distant. 'Lovely to see you again.' He turns to me, holding my gaze a moment longer than necessary. 'Temperance. Thank you again.'

I watch him walk away, unable to breathe fully until he climbs into his truck. Then I turn to Maxine.

'That man,' she remarks, shaking her head. 'I'm not sure he has any idea how damn attractive he is.'

I almost choke. I'm pretty sure the man who used his body to turn mine into a traitor knew *exactly* what he was doing.

The noise I make is not remotely convincing, and Maxine taps my arm. 'You can't be serious. Everyone in this town knows Kade is the nicest bloke going around, *and* he's got the best ass.'

Laughing, I shake my head, though a small pinch tightens under my ribs. 'Would you ...?' I venture.

She lifts a perfect brow. 'Go there?' She checks her nails. 'Once, maybe. But not now. He is most definitely not interested.'

We step out of the walkway and catch up: her weddings, the weekend she'll spend at the lake near my parents, and how I still don't have a rider for the upcoming competitions.

'Maybe you should advertise or something?' Maxine suggests.

The idea makes my skin crawl. It would mean publicly admitting defeat, and I can already imagine Walter Wilder pinning the ad to his damn wall to laugh at every day. No. Better to slink away quietly.

My throat tightens.

Bree's healing well, and Ryan's being great, making sure she's got everything she needs. But we both really needed her to ride, and that loss is going to sting for a long while.

Chapter Ten

TEMPERANCE

Marlowe's found me a rider. An actual fucking rider, and I can't believe it. The only nagging worry is that she won't tell me anything about them. No name. No competition history. Nothing specific. Just that they're an established horseperson with experience in Nightshade's disciplines – reining, and reined cow horse. Someone who understands, and can take a skilled horse through, the precise manoeuvres that create a controlled reining pattern in the arena; and then let the horse's cow sense and instincts take over to work a cow. Both require an immense amount of skill, and a kind of oneness between horse and rider which, apparently, this person has. And, supposedly, they have a reputation for a gentle approach – which is absolutely non-negotiable for me – and they're interested in riding Nightshade.

There are a lot of potential upsides.

Other than sounding like the perfect rider, she told me I need to reserve judgement.

Obviously, that's the bit that worries me the most. Why would I need to reserve judgement? We're talking about someone – other than Bree – who might ride my most prized possession. Judgement is everything.

But Nightshade is so much more than that. More than a possession. He's my hopes and dreams wrapped up in a well-proportioned, athletic, shiny – at least when he's freshly groomed – package. Even if he wasn't the last foal my grandfather ever bred, I'd have loved him with everything I have. Nightshade was born at the height of Riverbow's struggles, saw my grandfather die, and my parents move away. He watched me try to rebuild our home with my hands literally in the dirt. And he nibbles my hair. He's my soul horse, and I'd kill anyone who tried to bring him harm.

That's who I'm supposed to be offering up to a stranger. Not to mention that, if they're as good as my non-rider-but-very-good-researcher friend claims, why aren't they already committed to another horse?

But if I want Gabe Archer's Riverbow Stud back on the reining circuit's radar, I need to put any reservations aside and at least meet them. Because once the reining community sees him run, I have no doubt Nightshade's offspring will be factored into the next five to ten years of their breeding plans.

I glance out at the paddock where I keep the mares and their foals. They're out of sight at the moment, just on the other side of the rise towards the river, and that suits me fine.

No one needs to know I have hopes for more horses than just Nightshade. He's the only one ready, anyway. Riverbow Stud is not a factory. We're – well, *I'm* – a well-planned, considered, and kind stud where horses are cherished, not treated as commodities. We don't treat our horses like the Wilders do. Even if it means the gap of success between the two once-equally matched patriarchs turned into a chasm, it will stay that way – I won't compromise my values.

As a large white truck rounds the bend, my stomach knots so tightly I press my palm to it, willing myself to settle. My phone chimes and I glance at it, mostly for something to do as the truck slows to a stop near the barn. The darkened windows give nothing away.

Marlowe: Give it a chance. Please. You deserve this. You both do.

The text does nothing to ease my nerves as the truck door shuts and boots thud softly across the dirt.

I look up. My heart lurches into my throat. The swirling knots in my gut become a fluttering chaos.

Kade fucking Wilder stands there, hat in hand, watching me warily.

Closing my eyes for a moment doesn't make him disappear.

She cannot be serious. Marlowe wants me to give *him* a chance on my horse? What the fuck was she thinking?

Kade slides the brim of his hat through his hands like he's steering a go-kart, a movement that makes me wonder if he's more nervous about being here than I'd have guessed. The thought bolsters me. Reminds me how those hands felt on my body as Juniper played her siren song, and how much I cannot have this man anywhere near me.

'Fuck no,' I snap, pointing at him. 'You can just get back in your truck and turn around.'

'Temperance,' he says gently, calmly, as he steps forward.

My name in his mouth drags a shiver from me. I swallow hard. Did he spike my gin with something that still hasn't left my system? Why does he have to be so damn attractive, his stupid voice raking over my skin? And why do I even notice?

Lucky he's a Wilder, and my head knows more than my treacherous body.

'Correct,' I confirm. 'Temperance *Archer*. Or did you forget who I am? Who this ranch used to belong to?'

His chest expands with an inhale, but he's not surprised. He hasn't forgotten a thing – he knew exactly how this would go. But he doesn't answer.

'Why are you here, Mr Wilder?' I ask, using his surname to remind myself who he is. To keep distance between us.

His dark blond brows pull down a fraction. 'Mr Wilder is my grandfather,' he replies in a low voice. 'Not me.'

There's a depth to that denial. One that doesn't sound full of pride.

'So what am I supposed to call you?' I counter. Stupid question. We both know I'm painfully aware of who he is.

He moves towards me slowly, the way someone approaches a spooked horse. I think of all the horses I've seen in my time. Maybe that *is* how I feel – fight or flight. And right now, I'm in fight. But if he gets too close ...

'Kade will do for now,' he says.

For now?

All my organs spin. What the fuck does that mean?

'He's even more beautiful up close,' he murmurs as he walks past me to the wooden fence of the round yard.

He goes to lean on the rail and I grab his arm.

'Don't,' I say, quickly letting go again. 'It ... needs work. You'll get splinters.'

I grit my teeth. I don't actually care if he gets splinters, but I don't need him seeing how much we've struggled since his grandfather swindled mine out of our best stud horses. Not to mention the boundary shift he coerced the council into making that meant the old cottage – which could have been a good source of revenue for Riverbow Ranch – now belongs to them.

And it just sits there. Deteriorating more with every rising sun.

My blood simmers, thinking of the photo in Kade's bar taken from the front of that cottage.

'It's fine,' he murmurs, still looking at Nightshade as he rests his forearms on the rail.

I try not to focus on how warm his arm was under my palm and instead try wishing him so many splinters they'd be impossible to remove. I stay where I am, letting my gaze linger on the breadth of his shoulders. How in the world am I going to get him to leave?

'Whatever Marlowe promised you, you can have it. Please, just leave.'

He dips his chin, looking over his shoulder at me, hat dangling from one hand on Nightshade's side of the yard.

'You don't even want to know what it would cost you? You want me gone that badly?'

'Yes,' I answer, ignoring the tiny voice that wonders what would happen if he rode Nightshade. Kade's reputation as a trainer has him at near god-like status in the entire Blackwood Valley region – from the lake to Whimsy Ridge, the city, and everything in between. I can only imagine how far that worship extends. But he's never ridden in a competition, so why now? He wants something. And whatever it is will leave me stripped of something I don't want to give.

'Why?' he asks, turning to face me. 'I thought you needed someone to ride him in a fortnight?' He jerks his thumb at Nightshade, who eats quietly from his feed bin, ears flicking towards us.

I laugh. 'Not you. I do *not* need you.'

He nods silently, but something flickers in his eyes. 'Me, or a Wilder?'

I gape at him. 'They're the same thing!'

'Incorrect, Temperance. Wilder may be my surname, but you know nothing more about me than that. Not once have I judged you based on the feud between our families, and yet, here you are, having done nothing but judge me since the fifth grade.'

He doesn't raise his voice, but the truth in it lands between my ribs. At the same time, everything I *do* know about him floods my mind as though it wants to prove him wrong. He never played sport at school, even though every team was desperate to have him; his grades were better than mine; I loathed the girlfriend he had in college who never seemed to make him truly smile; he's got a great laugh; and he feels—

Shit, Temperance. Focus.

'Give me one good reason I shouldn't judge you for your family's sins,' I grind out.

Kade stares at me for so long I have to force myself to hold his gaze and will the flush from my cheeks. Then he turns back to the railing and scales it before I find the wherewithal to understand what just happened. He jumps from the top, landing on the sand and moving slowly towards Nightshade, the horse's attention now completely on Kade.

My heart races. Part of me wishes Nightshade would flatten his ears at Kade's approach. Make it known how much he is not welcome here.

But I know my horse better than that. He's curious, and he loves a challenge.

And the man swaggering his way across the round yard is presenting a big fucking challenge to both of us.

Nightshade snuffs at him, nostrils flaring gently.

'I know, I know. She doesn't want me here, so you wanna take her lead, huh?' I can hear Kade saying softly to the black stallion. I frown at his back. 'But we'll show her we can be a team, right? You'll help me, won't you, big guy?'

To my disgust, Nightshade nudges Kade's stomach as soon as he reaches his side.

Surely he has treats in his shirt pocket.

I grip the timber railing, splinters be damned, and watch Kade slowly place his right hand on Nightshade's neck. He strokes towards Nightshade's shoulder as his left hand rests on my horse's nose. Nightshade's nostrils flare slightly under the edge of Kade's hand, but Kade doesn't stop stroking. He brushes his palms over the stallion's short hair, left hand now running the top ridge of Nightshade's neck as he moves around him. For a moment, Nightshade flicks his ears back and lifts his head high as Kade nears his hindquarters. But as Kade continues to murmur and stroke, never losing contact with the horse as he works his way around the full length of his body, Nightshade's head slowly lowers. His breath huffs as he eventually drops his head to Kade's chest height, ears and eyes softening as he settles into the rub-down.

After several long moments – and some unwanted loosening in my own chest – Kade reaches for the saddle and bridle I'd put on the fence earlier. After saddling him, Kade runs Nightshade slowly through some warm-ups and then a simple reining pattern. His seat is good, and Nightshade is relaxed under the loose rein, ears flicking back every now and then as if checking what Kade might ask of him next.

As he completes the reining pattern, the sand dust still settling after an incredible sliding stop, I lower my forehead to the timber.

Because, best I can tell, that run would have got a perfect damn score.

Chapter Eleven

KADE

I feel like I'm soaring. The black stallion beneath me is nothing but grace and power, the exact shape of my hopes and dreams on the circuit.

I knew he'd be good. Old man Archer knew his horses and, if Temperance has learned even half of what he could teach her, the bloodlines she's building will be impeccable. Still, I ride incredible horses every day, and Nightshade has outstripped them in one practice run.

Making a name for myself on a Wilder horse was the ideal scenario – I'd be freed from the obscurity of the 'Wilder Inc.' that gets listed on the *trained by* section of the reining entries. I'd finally be stepping out from under my grandfather's influence without giving up everything – my name, my parents' legacy, and the inheritance I need to support Cami. I would've walked away a hundred times over if doing so didn't mean leaving with nothing to show for all the years we've spent in that house.

In my bones, I know our mother would never have wished for us to be raised as we were. But all it took was one inattentive driver, and what she and my father wanted no longer mattered. We were under the 'care and guidance' of a ruthless man for all of our formative years. Even now, the hold he has—

But if I can't do it for my mother and Cami on Wilder horses, I can carry our name and do it on someone else's. It might mean losing access to the horses I've trained, but if I can help us this way instead, the money I could make from training and riding other horses – along with the steady income from Meadow and Velvet – can still support Cami.

And this stallion – Nightshade – is it. He's how I get there. He's our ticket. I can feel it.

I glance over to where Temperance watches, eyes narrowed, morning sunlight dancing in her hair. I'm not surprised she didn't know it was me Cami and Marlowe teed up to come today. Had she known, she would've cancelled – or shot me on sight for trespassing.

My guess is the latter.

After a few more goes around the arena, I lope him over to Temperance. Not because I needed the extra runs to know he's it for me, or that I'll do *everything* in my power to make her agree, but because riding him feels like something I'll never get enough of.

'Are you done with him for today?' I ask, swinging my leg over and stepping to the ground, before gently looping the reins over the fence.

There's a pause, as though she's deciding how much she's willing to give. 'Yes.'

We look at each other across the railing, the space between us crackling with something I can't read – something that could go a lot of ways.

'Don't say it,' she warns.

I blink. 'Say what?'

'I could see it, okay,' she bites out. 'I don't want to know how it felt for you up there. You're a great rider, Kade, sure. But you're not *my* rider.'

My head goes a little fuzzy at the vehemence behind *not my rider*, but it's not enough to eclipse the jolt low in my gut when she uses my first name.

I turn to the stallion standing quietly beside me and undo his cinch, lowering the thick strap under his belly. After hefting the saddle off his back and hanging it on the fence, I return to collect the saddle blanket.

'Okay,' I concede. 'I'm not *your* rider. But I'm pretty sure I'm *his*.'

'No.'

Stroking Nightshade's spine, I figure it's now or never. I need to get back to Wilder Station, but I can't leave without knowing where she stands.

'Listen, Temperance,' I say without looking at her. 'We both need this. I want to ride, and he's the horse I need to show what I can do. I'm an excellent match for his skill and you know it. You've got the best fucking horse in the region – one who could go all the way to Nationals *and* be the number-one stud pick in a hundred-thousand-mile radius. You need him visible on the circuit, crushing it. And to do that, you need me.'

I hear the air rush from her lungs and turn to face her, the fence between us.

'Let's be real, Temperance,' I say quietly. 'Can you afford another year here if you miss this round?'

The truth is, I don't know her financial situation. I know she works damn hard, and her flower business seems to be going well, but even a cursory glance around the farm tells me things could be better. And, unfortunately, I'm all too aware of what my grandfather's accusations did to Gabe Archer's stud.

Her jaw clenches as she assesses me, mind clearly full of warring thoughts. My pulse hammers as I watch her work it through. She's got the faintest dusting of freckles across her forehead and cheekbones. I've never seen them before – probably from all the outdoor work – and I shove the impulse to trace them into a dark corner of my mind.

As I picture her in the flower fields I saw around the other side of the house, another idea sparks. But discussing any other possible collaborations isn't worth the energy if she won't even consider the one she needs so badly.

Finally, she takes a brush from the bucket at her feet and hands it to me, but doesn't let go. Her hand stays in mine, the brush caught between our palms as she glares at me.

'I have tried to be civil about you and your family my entire life,' she says. 'Can I afford another year here without the stud? No. Because your grandfather lied, took what didn't only belong to him, and ruined my family in the process. You know as well as I do that your top horses come from bloodlines my grandfather put together and was never remunerated for. He was pushed out as someone who mistreated horses, which couldn't be further from the truth. And don't even get me started on the cottage that just sits rotting on the edge of your land. Walter Wilder *stole* my time here, Kade.'

I cup her hand, tightening my grip slightly, and she draws a sharp inhale. I know that's what they believe, and it's not entirely wrong. I know better than anyone the lengths my grandfather will go to get what he wants. But on this issue, I've seen the papers. The stallion her grandfather claimed he bought with mine was purchased solely with Wilder money. I don't condone my grandfather going against whatever agreement they had in place – actions that meant the Wilders went on to bigger and supposedly better things, while the Archers struggled for everything they ever had. And I certainly don't condone that he drugged horses. But did Gabe really have no idea?

The money trail is what it is. And Temperance's view doesn't account for all the work I've done on the horses that came after.

As for the cottage ...

'I'm sorry,' I murmur, closing my hand around hers a little more. Just enough pressure to show I mean it. Pressure that lets the heat of her skin bleed into mine.

Her face drops, like she can't quite believe what I've said but refuses to let it show.

'I owe you nothing,' she grinds out. 'And I will live on the back of that horse if he's all I have left, because I'll give up this ranch before I let myself be fucked over by a Wilder. You will never stop proving yourself to me. I'll give you *one* opportunity to show this is about what you've said, not some elaborate scam to continue the Wilders' domination of Blackwood Valley and beyond. The second I feel my interests aren't upheld, I'll pull Nightshade from you faster than you can blink.'

She pushes the brush into my hand and points behind me. 'Turn him out in that paddock when you're done and – so help me – if your actions bring Walter's attention to me, you *will* regret it.'

I can only stare after her, the brush limp in my hand as I watch her ass walk away. Temperance Archer has a bite.

And I fucking like it.

Jamie ruffles my hair before gently pushing at my head as we take our seats around his fairy-light-filled fire pit.

Cami laughs. 'I knew you would charm her!'

Jamie cocks an eyebrow at me and, for the first time, I wonder how much he saw that night at the bar. I look away before he can drop me in anything in front of Cami.

'I didn't charm her,' I reply, wondering why those words feel so disappointing. 'I'm pretty sure I'm lucky she didn't shoot me in the face.'

'Yeah,' Cami says, 'that would be because Marlowe agreed it was best we didn't tell her who you were.'

'But you got the gig?' Jamie asks from where he now sits on the other side of the fire, nursing a beer.

Did I get the gig? I've been asking myself that since I drove away after brushing down Nightshade and putting him in the paddock, Temperance nowhere in sight.

'I think ... I've got a shot at the gig,' I say. 'I think I'm in, if I can keep proving myself to her.'

Cami nods, settling back into her canvas chair next to me. 'Makes sense,' she murmurs. 'We know how much you're up against here, but you can do this.' She reaches out and squeezes my forearm. 'You deserve an opportunity to ride, Kade. He can't keep that from you. He won't give it to you, so you need to fight for it another way.'

I smile at her. The faith my little sister has in me makes my heart feel like it's doubling in my chest.

'I don't have a plan yet on how to manage him,' I admit, the weight of it pressing down on my shoulders.

She places a hand on my forearm. 'We keep it to ourselves for now, and then we do it like everything else. Together.'

'How do we make sure you keep "proving" yourself?' Jamie asks.

Sighing, I shake my head. That's the bit I've been wracking my mind over. The riding bit is easy.

Temperance Archer is a whole other game.

Chapter Twelve

TEMPERANCE

The flurry in my stomach as Kade gets out of his truck well after sundown is getting harder and harder to ignore. Not only is he an incredible rider who's been able to smooth out some of Nightshade's minor quirks, speed up his lead changes, and lengthen his sliding stops, but he's even calmer and gentler than Bree when he works.

Nightshade preens under his tutelage, and the war it creates in my body is like nothing I've ever experienced. The evidence of how well they're doing fights for purchase against the reality of who he is, and what his family took from mine.

'Hey,' he says, making his way over in the dark.

Looking the way he does, and clearly being exceptionally skilled in the reining world, gin making, and driving the success of Meadow and Velvet, you'd think he'd be more arrogant. He certainly exuded a 'fuck off' vibe to most people at school. Jameson and Camilla were about the only ones he seemed to genuinely associate with, never mind the girlfriends I couldn't stand. But the arrogance I expected him to have in spades? It doesn't seem to exist.

Instead, he has a quiet, steady confidence with Nightshade – an assurance that seems to settle every concern the horse might have before it even begins.

And it's a warmth that feels dangerously close to spilling over onto me as well.

My gaze slides up his thick, jean-clad thighs as he comes closer to the round yard. The light he brought over illuminates him in a way that makes him look like a golden god walking out of the darkness, and my skin tingles. He stops beside me and we both watch Nightshade, who's clearly waiting for his nightly ride.

His schedule, at least what I've pieced together, is brutal. He works with his station horses in the early hours, is at Meadow and Velvet until after dinner, then comes here. I'd bet good money that after riding Night-shade, he heads straight back to the bar to finish up.

I stifle a yawn courtesy of my own schedule – up early to feed and check my horses, then all day in the garden or with Maxine or a client. Part of me wants to go to bed and leave them to it, but a larger part refuses to be a person who trusts a Wilder.

'Sorry these rides are so late,' he says quietly, glancing over his shoulder at me.

'I'm as happy to keep this under wraps as you seem to be,' I reply, with a little more bite than he probably deserves now that he's been at this for the best part of a week and a half. *But there's still time to pull out*, I remind myself. I don't have to register him and Nightshade as a pair for another forty-eight hours.

He makes a low sound in his throat as he watches Night-shade. 'Yeah. Safe to say if Walter finds out too soon, it'll be ... tricky.' He looks back at me. 'I think we should give him the night off.'

I glance up at him. 'Why?'

'So he has enough in the tank for the first round,' he says simply. 'We both know what he can do. Now he knows what I can do, and that's about all there is to it this close to competition time.'

I study his profile – the slight sadness at the corners of his mouth, the shadows hollowing his cheeks. Something tugs in my chest. Somehow, between the morning of Juniper's last hometown gig and now, standing in the dark with Kade, I've become ... curious. Sometimes more than curious.

It's a feeling I know I shouldn't have, but compared to some of the more recent feelings he stirs in me, it's the safest one.

'Why are you really doing this?' I ask. 'Your grandfather would hardly approve of you sullying your name here.'

He doesn't look at me this time, but I see his shoulders drop slightly as he exhales.

'Have a drink with me,' he says.

It's not a question. It's a quiet command wrapped in sincerity so disarming that saying 'no' doesn't even cross my mind until far too late. Even then, I just nod and head for the house.

He follows in silence. If the sound of his boots didn't give it away, the fact that my body feels alive in a way it never has before would. Somehow, I just *know* he's watching the way I walk – and damn it if I can't help but sway my hips a little more than normal. Just a touch.

I pause at the kitchen door, fingers around the handle while I try to calibrate what it'll feel like having him in my space. Maybe I shouldn't invite him in. Make him do another run on Nightshade and leave it at that.

But I know as well as he does that a night off won't hurt my horse, and we could use the time to make sure Kade is up to speed on the patterns. Talent and hard work are one thing, but if you stuff the pattern, you zero out on the reining anyway.

My mind has also snagged on the way he didn't defend Walter. Why is he really prepared to do this with my horse? Surely I'm getting the better deal out of this arrangement than Kade is.

He steps up behind me, and my mind flashes back to that night in his bar, my whole body warming from the inside out.

We stand there for a moment – me staring at the door that needs painting, thrumming with anticipation at his closeness, yet completely unable to turn around. Unable to look into the face of the man whose presence is throwing me so completely off balance.

Kade runs the back of his fingers along my tricep and my breath hitches.

'Are you going to let me in?' he asks, and I close my eyes against the timbre of his voice.

'Temperance,' he murmurs, stepping closer, his front almost flush against my back. 'You don't have—'

I spin, facing him fully now, looking up into his blue eyes, his face lit by the sensor light I had installed.

'Why are you really doing this?' I breathe, his chest so close I could grip his shirt if I wanted. I make a fist at my side instead. How have I gone from hating him to vibrating in his presence in less than a fortnight?

'With Nightshade?' he asks, voice thick.

'With me.' Heat floods my cheeks the moment the words escape, but there's no way he doesn't know exactly what I mean. 'I know Nightshade's the best, but you have other very talented horses on your station.'

I had, truly, intended to ask in terms of Nightshade – but the truth behind my question remains the same. And the way he towers over me, presses me gently towards the door, smiles with pride after an amazing run on Nightshade, the way he held me at the bar ... the concern at the market when I hit my head, and his kindness at the bakery – I'm not imagining any of it.

He shoves his hands in his pockets but steps even closer. Close enough my breasts almost brush him.

'Two reasons,' he whispers. 'One, you unravelled something in my storeroom and somehow you're still holding the other end of the rope. And two, you gave me a shot at something I never thought I'd have. Something you had every right to deny me.'

I swallow. 'I would have been denying myself as well.' The words barely make it out, my head spinning.

'You would have found another way,' he replies, tipping his head towards mine. 'I've watched you a long time, Temperance Archer. Nothing beats you.'

'My grandfather's death almost did.'

The confession slips out before I can stop it, and I can't help the tears that follow. I don't know why I've blurted it out, but something in the way Kade is looking at me makes me want to do two impossible things at once: remind him why he should back off, and show him my most painful pieces, just so he'll soothe them. Let him talk to me gently, the way he talks to Nightshade. Like I'm powerful and precious.

Kade cups my cheek, and I let my head rest back against the door as I look up at him. His brows draw together, a whirl of emotions twisting across his features.

A gentle throb starts between my legs as warmth pools low in my belly. His pink mouth is almost close enough to kiss, and my hands skim his chest, resting lightly there. My fingers tremble against his pale green shirt.

His thick fingers slide just beyond my hairline beneath my ear, goosebumps rippling across my skin. My hands drift higher on his chest as I study his lips, imagining their heat against mine. Imagining his tongue—

Kade brushes his thumb across my mouth and my breath hitches, my gaze flying to his.

I open to mouth to say something – *anything* – but nothing comes. I'm silently begging him to kiss me. Gently, he slips his thumb inside my mouth and I wrap my lips around the tip. His eyelids go heavy and—

Kade curses as his phone rings.

My heart finally catches up, pounding wildly as the fog in my mind clears. What the fuck was I about to do? With *Kade*?

His phone keeps ringing, cutting through the quiet of my farm and shattering whatever spell we were weaving. I grip his wrist and ease his hand from my face, unable to look away as I do. *He's a Wilder*, I remind myself fiercely, wishing he seemed more like the version of them I carry in my mind. But what would my family say if they knew what I was doing? Nightshade is one thing – but *this*?

Letting his wrist go, I open the door behind me, step inside, and shut him out.

Chapter Thirteen

KADE

'Fuck, fuck, *fuck*,' I curse, slamming the back of my head into the headrest.

I twist my hands around the steering wheel, trying to work out what the hell to do now. There's no way Temperance didn't pick up on how desperate I was – *am* – to feel her mouth on mine. She clearly knows it's no longer only Nightshade keeping me coming back night after night.

If I'm honest, it didn't start out as solely Nightshade, either. I told her she unravelled something in me – a truth I never imagined sharing with her. But now that it's out, I can't imagine how I'd ever cram it back in. Despite how much I should.

The shrill ring of my phone cuts through the dark cab, and I clear my throat. 'Hey, Cami.'

'What's wrong? You sound strange,' she says.

'Nothing. Just ... a misunderstanding with Temperance.'

She's quiet for a beat. 'One you can sort out?'

'Ah ... I hope so, yeah.' The words are more reflex than anything.

I hate lying to Cami, but she was so excited about this opportunity. She even moved to the B&B, for fuck's sake. And I have no idea what happens now with Temperance and me – it's likely she won't let me within a hundred yards of her front gate ever again.

'Was the misunderstanding on her end or yours?' Cami asks.

I hesitate, thinking of the way her hands slid up my chest. 'Both?'

'Well … our families have always had a relationship with the colour grey. Can you make it a little more black and white for her?'

I laugh. Pretty sure I did that.

But I need to backtrack on this, and quickly. The last thing I need is to add fuel to Temperance's fire by proving every suspicion she has about the Wilders. I've already pushed her too far on something that would be much easier if we kept a very clear boundary.

'You can sort this out,' Cami insists, her voice chipper. 'She hasn't shot you yet, I assume, so just get back on the horse—'

My phone chimes in my ear. I check it, losing the thread of her pep talk as I pull the phone away.

Temperance has sent me a photo.

My ears ring as I open it. Nightshade's registration for the first qualifying ride – with me listed as his rider.

Holy shit.

I can't help but smile as my chest tightens, and I lift the phone back to my ear. Whatever I need to do about my attraction to her, I want to ride Nightshade.

'I'll sort it,' I tell Cami.

I think I might be sick.

Reining and reined cow horse competitions – even when the cow component is secondary – are supposed to be adrenaline-fuelled, precise, and reaffirming. All of which they are when I'm watching. But today – the day Temperance and I travel across the county to the first major qualifying event – I feel ill. I can't tell if it's because this will be my first proper competitive ride, or because of the woman sitting silently beside me in my truck.

Or the fact that, today, my grandfather will see me as a traitor – openly – for the first time. Today, I officially give up all links to the horses I've spent years working with. Not that Temperance isn't deserving, but I never considered I'd be doing it because of an Archer. Or at all.

I've got you, whatever happens, Cami had said before we left, the women exchanging small smiles – Temperance's tight compared to Cami's nervous one. I send up a silent thank you that despite everything that's happened, and despite the man who raised us, I was blessed with my sister.

'You okay?' Temperance asks, breaking the silence of the last several hours.

I glance sideways at her, keeping my focus on the road and the fact that I'm towing her very valuable horse in my gooseneck. She wanted to bring him herself, but somehow, during our stilted text conversations, I managed to convince her we should take my truck and trailer with its sleeping quarters.

I'll bring my swag, she'd texted.

'Kade,' she says softly when I don't respond.

My knee bounces and I press my palm down my thigh before resting it on the gear shift.

'I'm fine,' I reply. 'Just some nervous energy – we've been cooped up in here for a while.'

'We can take a break whenever you need,' she says gently. 'I'm always ready for coffee.'

I drive in silence again for the next few minutes, acutely aware Temperance seems to be stewing on something beside me. I still haven't worked out the best way to de-escalate what I started if she raises it and, while part of me knows I should take the lead, I can't bring myself to shut it down either.

She's staring out the window when I glance at her, so I can't see her face. Is she finally going to call me out about almost kissing her?

Instead, her hand finds mine on the gear shift, and I suck in a breath at the contact.

'Kade,' she begins, and I spread my fingers so hers slip between them as if it's the most natural thing in the world. Then I close them – gripping hers – and hold her hand where it cups over mine.

The sensation mimics itself in the centre of my chest, like whatever hold she has on me is only tightening, no matter what logic I throw at it.

'I know you're not like him,' she says, voice barely a whisper. 'You can do this – make your own name.'

The warmth of her skin is intoxicating, but not more so than her words. They're what pulse through me and flood my veins with something I've never experienced. Something hot and overwhelming that tightens my throat.

We stay like that for a long time, driving down the straight, barren highway with nothing between us but our held hands.

The event venue is teeming with people, trucks, floats, goosenecks, and horses, as we drive through the wide entry marked with two sandstone pillars. A timber sign hanging high between them reads *Wentworth Station*.

I exhale and glance at Temperance, who nods at me.

We both know there's no coming back from this in so many ways. Plenty of people will have already seen my name listed against her horse, but I've managed to avoid anyone who might question me on it. My grandfather, though – he knows. I'm sure of it. And – my stomach sinks – he'll make his displeasure known in whatever way causes the most damage. I know it.

'We're over here, I think.' Temperance points to the left of the covered arena, along a row of camp sites large enough for me to park the rig and set us up for the two nights we're here.

Once we've stabled Nightshade and made sure he's settled, and made our various small-talk rounds – separately – I wait for Temperance at our site. The smell of the simple vegetarian camp nachos I've made for her permeates the air, and I find myself hoping hard that she likes nachos.

It's almost completely dark when she returns, squinting slightly into the lights running the length of the truck, a light layer of dust on her dark jeans.

'You made dinner?' she asks, lifting her brows.

'Just something basic. Hopefully it's edible.'

She takes a seat at the small table I've set up outside, dragging her plastic bowl towards her and peeling back the foil on her nacho parcel. Steam curls up into her face and she laughs.

'God, it smells so good,' she says. 'I'm starving.'

Watching Temperance eat is mesmerising – almost as good as watching her drink my gin. When she twirls a piece of stringy cheese around her finger and pops it into her mouth, I have to look away and force myself to focus on my own food.

'How do you think he's going to go overnight?' I ask.

She folds up her empty foil and drops the ball back in her bowl. 'Honestly? He's going to get more rest than either of us. We'll need to watch his nerves around the arena – there's so many new things around there – but right now he's living his best life in that stable with hay on demand.' She shakes her head, smiling. 'Although he'd probably prefer to be closer to the mares.'

Stroking my beard, I think through how to approach that with him tomorrow. Make sure he's not too skittish. I study her as I do. 'You're nervous?'

'I'm not nervous about your run,' she answers without hesitation, and I can't help but smile. 'But yeah – I'm nervous about how he'll be received. Will they see what I see? Or will they just see the Archer name and not give me a shot?'

Her honesty is like a glass of cool water – something I didn't realise how much I needed. So much of my life has been planning, strategising, hiding – at least outside of Cami and Jamie. This is ... new. And welcome.

'Who'd have thought the three of us would end up newbies together?'

She laughs and I join her. 'Definitely not me,' she says. 'Not so long ago, I almost told Marlowe I wanted to bury a hatchet in your chest.' Her cheeks colour as she glances at me, like she didn't mean to let that slip.

I gape at her. 'Holy shit. You did not!'

A smile creeps across her face. 'I did. Maybe your grandfather isn't so wrong about my family being the worst of the worst, right?'

The cheek in her tone makes my heart thump a little harder. 'I try to believe he's not the best judge of character.'

'Well, we've already established he got you wrong, so we can definitely agree on that.'

'So ... you're not going to hack me to pieces in my sleep?'

This time, her laugh is louder, unrestrained. She purses her lips as if considering it. 'Maybe only after your first ride gets my horse noticed. Then anything is fair game.'

She stands abruptly, placing her bowl in the plastic bucket I've set out for the washing up. 'Anyway,' she murmurs, looking away, 'time for me to wash up and find somewhere to sleep.'

I push away the flicker of disappointment that she's cutting our dinner short, but I get it. Being here with me – now publicly attached to her prize stallion – would be a lot.

It's a lot for me.

Clearing the rest of our dinner and stacking the dirty plates to wash with the breakfast dishes, I run tomorrow's reining pattern through my mind. The circles, the spins, the number of stops. Nightshade knows the technical components of each, credit for which goes almost entirely to the young trainer, Bree. When – *if* – I'm ever running the station myself, I might see whether she wants to join the team.

'Shit,' Temperance says behind me, where she's dragged her swag out of storage.

'Okay?' I ask over my shoulder.

'Ah ... yeah ...'

I wipe my hands on the towel and turn to see her staring at her swag, looking like she's weighing up her next move.

I frown and walk over. 'What is it?'

She looks up, her cheeks pinker than I've ever seen them, searching my face. 'It's fine,' she mutters, without a shred of conviction. 'It's – it's just wet.'

'What's wet?'

'My swag. I just spilled – look, don't worry, I'm good. I'll just—'

As what she's saying – and not saying – dawns on me, I shove my hands in my pockets. 'Temperance, are you telling me you'd prefer to sleep on the *ground*, in a *soggy swag*, than in a clean, dry bed?'

'Well, no …'

'No …' I step closer, my body pulled towards her of its own accord, just like that night at her door. 'You're saying you'd prefer *that* over being in close quarters with me.'

If she needs an out, this is the best I can offer. She flounders, clutching the rolled, damp swag to her chest like it'll protect her from me.

'Or …' I continue when she doesn't respond, closing the distance again, 'are you realising you *would* in fact like a clean, dry bed … but that there's only *one*?'

Chapter Fourteen

TEMPERANCE

I really need Kade to take that sinful smile off his face. As it is, I'm already heady from his proximity and the way he makes me laugh. How it felt to share the nachos he cooked for me. How what I said to Marlow about the hatchet actually entertained him. And not in a condescending way – more like I'd impressed him somehow. Not that Wilders are impressed by anything except what they can take.

But add that fucking smile that makes his eyes sparkle and crinkle at the edges, and all my lady parts think it's party time.

'I'm not sleeping with you,' I whisper fiercely, suddenly hyperaware of the other campers around us. We've already attracted the skin-burning attention I expected; I do *not* need to add fuel to a rumour.

He quirks a brow, his face altogether too close to mine. 'I gathered that when you literally locked me out.' He pauses, scanning my face as if working something out. 'I'm sorry about that night, though,' he says, and I draw back a little. 'I didn't – I didn't mean to make you uncomfortable. I just—' He clears his throat and steps back. 'Anyway, sorry.'

I blink at him. Partly stunned at an apology from a Wilder, partly disappointed in myself that I didn't expect it from him. That I underestimated him because of his name.

But also … I didn't actually *want* an apology.

That's the bit that worries me the most.

I sigh, looking down at my rolled swag – the one I didn't close properly, letting my water bottle leak through. I *could* still sleep in it, technically. But do I want to? The chill is settling in, and tomorrow will be a huge day for us. Plus, the way Kade's fists slowly clench and unclench, almost in time with the tick in his jaw, doesn't exactly paint the picture of someone relaxed about what's ahead, even if he managed to hide it – or push it aside – over dinner.

I think about how the tension in his hand seemed to melt when I held it in the truck. Really, I owe it to Nightshade to make sure Kade isn't unnecessarily anxious for tomorrow.

'So,' I say, dumping the increasingly heavy swag back into the tack room of his trailer, 'just how clean is this bed of yours?'

He gives me a long look – one I feel all the way to my toes – before turning and climbing the short foldable stairs into the float.

I follow, pausing just inside. I knew the gooseneck was high-quality when we loaded Nightshade, but the living quarters are … well, they scream money. Not in an ostentatious way, in a horses-are-expensive-and-this-is-the-life-I-chose kind of way. Still, it's a life I could never afford.

Unless my stud …

I peek up to find him squeezing the back of his neck, as if adjusting to the fact that I'm clearly assessing everything.

There's a queen bed built over the hitch, and a little kitchenette with a table in the space we're standing in. The space that's suddenly full of the reality that I'm sharing it with Kade – someone I thought I hated. *Should* hate. And yet I look forward to seeing him every day. To sharing my horse with him. To the way he … understands that I want more for myself than what my family – despite not being at fault – left me with.

'Very clean,' he remarks, answering my earlier question with a sideways glance. 'I look after what's mine. I can take the swag.'

I stare at him before a nervous laugh bubbles up, heat flushing through me.

'No,' I say – meaning the swag. But also needing to remind myself his comment about looking after what's his was *not* meant for me. No way the thought of belonging to him in any way should create the kind of physical reaction that hits between my ribs – and my thighs. *But that's all it is*, I tell myself. A chemical response to being in close quarters with an annoyingly attractive man. Bodies have needs, and clearly I've been neglecting mine.

'No,' I repeat, surveying the floor. 'There's plenty of room down here. I can just—'

'Temperance,' he says firmly. 'I am not having you sleep on the floor of my truck in a wet fucking swag. I realise

I'll never fully prove myself to you, but I'm actually a gentleman.'

He looks genuinely put out when I glance up, a faint dusting of pink along his cheekbones above where his beard starts.

I stare at him, only a foot between us, my face burning as I start to accept what we're about to do. At the same time, my heart twists a little that he thinks I still hold that view of him. Not that I gave him any reason to think differently, considering how I reacted when he turned up as my 'surprise rider'.

'Right,' I say, looking him straight in those piercing blue eyes. 'Well, I can't have you on Nightshade less than perfect. So, it looks like we're sharing.'

He watches me for a moment, as if waiting for me to back out, before giving a short nod and stepping towards the bed.

I grip his forearm, stopping him. The muscles flex beneath my fingers, and I swallow.

'Kade,' I murmur, 'I know you're a gentleman.'

Retrieving our bags from the truck, we take turns changing while the other waits outside, and I say a quiet thank you to past me for packing with the swag in mind. The long, plain, pale blue sleep set is both comfortable and practical, with cuffs at the ankles so the legs don't ride up and no unnecessary skin showing. Therefore, there can be no accidental skin-to-skin contact as I share the bed with someone who, just a few short weeks ago, I would have called an enemy and is now ... someone I find myself thinking about – a little too positively – far more often than I'd like to admit.

Kade, on the other hand, is looking fucking delectable in soft black-and-white sleep shorts and a dark grey T-shirt stretched across his chest and shoulders. The fabric clings just enough to show the roundness of his shoulders and the upper definition of his pecs before it loosens, leaving the rest to my imagination.

An imagination currently running amok, wondering whether he has chest hair, tattoos, or any other markings I haven't yet seen. A little shiver runs through me – down towards my belly button, lower – as I wonder what it would feel like—

I press the pads of my fingers into my palm, as if rubbing away the phantom sensation of Kade's chest, and notice he's watching me expectantly.

'Sorry, pardon?' I ask.

He cocks his head. 'Do you want to pick a side?' he says, gesturing to the bed.

I look stupidly at it as I pull my hair off my neck and twist it into a loose, high ponytail. 'Ah ... the right?'

He nods and climbs onto the bed, crawling towards the left-hand side, and I watch his perfect fucking ass move away from me, wondering how on earth I'm meant to leave this sleeping arrangement unscathed.

I wait until he's settled before crawling up after him, positioning myself as far to the right as possible. It means one side of my body is pressed against the wall, but the mattress is so comfortable I don't think it will matter. The weight of the last few weeks settles over me as I lie still in his bed, our looming debut just around the corner.

A very public, irreversible statement of an arrangement between us.

How many people will pity me for repeating the mistakes of my family? Will they think I should have known better?

They'd be right.

And yet, here I am. Hyperaware of the muscular man beside me, feeling like my skin is tingling. The mattress dips as he settles, and a quiet longing unfurls in my chest. What would it be like to sleep beside someone every night?

The idea of it being Kade is impossible to escape as the warmth of him filters across the bed, my senses muddled by the scent of sandalwood and leather. I can't help but think about how he held my hand in the truck when I'd reached for him on instinct. There hadn't been any hesitation on his side either.

Minutes stretch into what feels like hours as my mind vacillates between rationalising why I'm here, worrying about tomorrow, and trying not to focus on how desperately I need Kade and Nightshade to go well.

His breathing is rhythmic and somehow emboldening. I want to touch him again – want to feel his skin slide beneath my palms. I roll onto my side to find him already doing the same.

Watching me.

His eyes are dark in the thin wash of ambient light in the sleeping quarters.

'Hey,' he murmurs, his voice thick, and I'm surprised he can't hear how hard my heart is beating – pumping a warmth that's pooling between my legs as I take in his shape. 'Can't sleep?'

My voice catches in my throat.

I shake my head instead.

'You know,' he whispers, his gaze boring through me, 'I'm really grateful you're here. That you've given me this chance despite it going against every instinct.'

Nodding slowly, I swallow. 'Yeah,' I breathe, 'my grandfather – who I respected immensely – would not be giving me encouraging words right now. Things were ... hard. After. I don't – I don't want to risk his ranch again.'

Kade blows out a breath. 'As far as I know, it's *your* ranch, Temperance. But I get that. And I'll do everything in my power to make sure it's never threatened.'

Watching him, the sincerity in his tone washing over me, I wonder what my instincts about him really are.

They're certainly not to hate him.

Chapter Fifteen

KADE

Temperance's legs are entwined with mine when she wakes. The same place they've been since just before the sun started to rise. The gentle sound of her breathing was calming in a way I hadn't realised something could be. I'd woken with a start, heart racing at the expectations of today – the uncertainty of whether my gamble will pay off, whether openly defying my grandfather after all these years won't just end in complete humiliation.

Watching Temperance sleep peacefully, her chest rising against my arm, made all of it seem more manageable somehow. As if her quiet breaths, the soft flutter of her eyelashes every now and then, brought clarity. Like I could tackle things bit by bit instead of drowning under the crushing sense of self-loathing and shame my relationship with him brings.

She stretches against me before she opens her eyes, her body moving instinctively. My dick thickens in response to the groan she makes deep in her throat as she presses gently into me, and I try to remind myself she's not actually aware of what she's doing yet.

Blinking in the soft sunlight streaming in the window behind me, she smiles – a small lift at the corners of her mouth that captures my attention immediately and makes me harder. I wonder what it would feel like to lick her there.

'Morning,' she murmurs shyly, a blush dusting the tops of her cheekbones. 'Did you sleep okay?' Her brows crease like she's just remembering we're here for me to ride her horse. Something she expects me to do well.

I swallow, and her frown deepens.

'You've got this, you know?' she says, and I just look at her, wondering how she can have such simple, focused faith in me. 'Kade?'

I smile, letting my hand trail down to her knee where it rests over my thigh, watching the blush creep further up her cheeks and around to her temples. She moves to pull away, the soft fabric sliding under my palm, and I grip gently, holding her in place.

'Yeah,' I reply, warmth pulling at my mouth. 'I've got this.'

She laughs and pushes lightly at my chest. 'It's good to see your swagger back.' She bops me on the nose, and I stare dumbly at her, at the way her throat moves with her laugh. Then seriousness settles over her features. 'But I'll support you when you're not sure too. We made a choice, and we stand by it.'

I can't help reaching out to cup the back of her head, drawing her towards me and pressing a kiss to her forehead. She gasps, her fingers digging slightly into my chest, but she doesn't move. I press a little harder before pulling away and dropping my head to hers, brushing the place I kissed and closing my eyes. My stomach swirls – part apprehension at her reaction, part something else entirely at the possibilities that might have just opened up.

We breathe against each other for long moments, my fingers in her hair, before I finally pull back to meet her gaze. Her eyes are slightly hooded as she slowly looks up at me, searching my face like she's looking for the same answers I am.

'I take it back,' I murmur. '*We've* got this.'

Nightshade is huffing and stamping in his stall when we reach him, and Temperance takes the lead going in, haltering him, and walking him out so we can warm him up. He throws his head about, likely in a heightened state with the new environment full of different sounds and smells, and the other horses – including mares – nearby.

We walk him around the station as the morning settles in, Temperance talking to him the entire time, often reaching out to stroke his neck until he finally starts to relax.

It's a gorgeous venue, set up specifically for events like this and filled with rows of stables, arenas of varying sizes, and expansive spaces for people to park their rigs and camp. When Wilder Station is mine, this green, accommodating layout is similar to what I'd want to create. Blackwood Valley township has a lot going for it, but a readily accessible, well-equipped horse venue is harder to find.

I push away the disappointment swimming in my gut as I think of the horses I've spent so much time with on the station. I've wanted this dream of riding for so long; I'm not prepared to give it up now.

It's more than that, though. On the surface, I'd be stupid to throw all of that away for one ride. But I'm also gaining some semblance of freedom from my grandfather. Not in the way I expected, but I'm taking something for me – something I've never done. And I'm being supported by people I love, like Cami and Jamie and – I glance at Temperance – by someone I never would have expected.

Someone who's also generating a warmth deep under my ribs I've never felt before.

'We're an hour and a half from your first run,' Temperance says, breaking me from my thoughts. 'We should get you on him, do some practice runs, make sure you're good with the pattern, and then rest him just before you go out.'

I swallow down the nerves that immediately charge through me and nod.

Watching Temperance lunge the stallion with such confidence and respect for him not only makes my pants feel tighter but creates a tangle in my chest. Forcing myself to focus on the horse and not the woman with auburn hair who is commanding more and more of my attention, I watch him move.

He's in good form today, responding well to Temperance's groundwork, and my veins start to fizz with excitement. I might not win today, and I don't have to – but I do need to qualify. Going down with nothing, and with no claim to Pix and the other Wilder horses, isn't an option. This will be the first of many rides with *my* name on the program. After this one, then I'll focus on winning. Right now, I want to ride the hell out of that black stallion.

Temperance walks beside Nightshade and me as we head down to the arena gates in preparation for my run. A competitor is just finishing, and the rider before me – a woman murmuring quietly to her buckskin horse, its head hung low – is already waiting. When she takes to the sand, I study her run: the lope is a good speed, her circles symmetrical, and her stops long and low.

Mine will be better.

I shift in the saddle and draw my shoulders back as I look down at Temperance. She smiles up at me before resting her hand on my knee. Her face pinkens, as if she hadn't quite meant to touch me so easily. Like it's something we do all the time.

'You've got this,' she declares, her hand trailing down the outside of my calf before she lets go.

Her faith in me is so genuine – pouring out of her so intensely, wrapping me in its warmth – that I almost miss the announcer calling my name.

'Next up,' the voice crackles through the speaker system, 'we have Kade Wilder on Night By Night We Walk. This is the first time either horse – owned by Temperance Archer of Riverbow Stud in Blackwood Valley – or rider have been on this arena.'

My heart thumps and I can't help but smile at Temperance – and to myself. Having Nightshade's stud name called, as with all the horses, sends a thrill through my veins.

Time to ride.

'Kade.' My grandfather's voice chills me as I pause halfway to the arena and he sidles up to the horse, completely unfazed that I could kick him in the face from here. He knows I won't.

'I will give you this ride,' he says, voice low. 'But you disrespect me like this again and it's more than those horses I'll take from you.'

He walks away, my world feeling like it's being dragged after him. *Call his bluff*, Jamie had said. I fucking hope we're ready for this. I watch him leave and gently squeeze Nightshade on.

In the moment, the run feels slow and steady, my heart pumping in my ears. I focus on the pattern – letting the country music spilling from the speakers fill my head – and give Nightshade his head and only the slightest instruction when he needs it. Breathing through the grip in my chest so he doesn't pick up on any nerves, I grin when he nails the lead change dead centre.

Probably unsurprisingly, my favourite parts of these runs are the stops. This pattern has three, and Nightshade lives for the speed as much as I do. Making our way towards the back corner of the arena, I line him up for a straight run parallel with the edge. It only takes a slightly firmer squeeze of my legs before he's off, his fast but graceful lope the easiest canter I've ever sat. For a moment, I think again that I'd pay well above average to get his first young trainer on my team somehow.

The end of the arena rushes towards us, Nightshade's nostrils flaring as he huffs for breath, and I sit back. 'Whoa,' I call firmly, sitting deep in the saddle and pressing my heels forward towards his shoulders – and only a fraction of a second later he's responding. His hindquarters drop low, his back hooves forging forward as he slides to a long, perfect stop.

Then we roll back, Night's shoulders rolling over his dropped hindquarters to lope in the opposite direction and do it again.

And again.

My cheeks hurt from smiling as I pause in the centre, nod to the judges, and pat Nightshade on the neck as we leave the arena. But it's the swelling in my chest that's almost overwhelming, searching for release. A laugh builds in my ribs but feels trapped somehow – until I find her in the crowd.

An auburn-haloed goddess whose hat is momentarily aloft as she grabs it and thrusts it in the air with a loud cheer. Her smile is aimed solely at me as the sun dances in her hair and across her face, illuminating her light.

I laugh but, at the same time, my throat thickens.

I think Temperance Archer might be ruining me. And she's not even trying.

Chapter Sixteen

TEMPERANCE

Elation is hot in my chest as Kade and Nightshade finish their run. It was fucking spectacular. The spins, the lead change, those stops ... my heart quickens as I remember how Kade looked, effortlessly sliding across the sand on my stallion.

The quiet that filled the arena when Kade was announced on my horse was enough to drop lead into my stomach. Then he started, and so did the murmurs. The appreciative looks.

And then Kade smiled at me, and there was no way I could contain my excitement – my hat in the air for just a moment, the same way my dad does. But now, all I can see is Kade swaggering towards me, Nightshade trailing behind him.

Nightshade's breaths are a little laboured, but he's recovering well as I'd expect of a horse in his condition. And he's relaxed, which I'd expect too, given his upbringing and his relationship with his rider.

My gaze drags over Kade. Over his boots dusted in a fine layer of sand and the gentle wrinkles at the hem of his jeans where they nearly meet the ground. Up over his thick thighs. My cheeks heat as I take in how well he fills out those jeans just below his gold and silver belt buckle, and then I track the blue check shirt stretched across his shoulders, the obvious bulge of his biceps.

The warm flush in my cheeks races south as I pass his throat and short beard and wonder what the texture of the hair there feels like.

'Eyes up here, Sundance,' he drawls as he reaches me.

The warmth completely overwhelms my system and I stare up at him, my pulse making itself known between my legs. Sundance? Since when does he have a nickname for me? And why is it so *hot*?

I will away all the inappropriate thoughts crystallising in my mind, but I still can't deny the compulsion to touch him, and I gently wrap my hand around his forearm.

'That was incredible,' I whisper, smiling up at him and feeling blinded by the one I receive in return.

He laughs. 'It *felt* incredible.'

Nightshade shifts behind him, and I let my hand drift down Kade's arm, fingers almost cupping his for longer than necessary before I step in and stroke Nightshade.

'You were incredible too,' I tell him.

'Oh my god, Kade,' a woman gushes, making both Nightshade and me flinch. I step back and bump into Kade's front in the process, his hand finding my hip for a moment – just like the night in his bar.

I hastily shuffle away, but not before I see the contact register on Camilla Wilder's face. Followed by the world's sliest grin.

Slowly, she looks at Kade, her face overtaken by a smile as big as his coming off the arena.

'Did you see your score?' she asks. 'You absolutely nailed it!'

Belatedly, I take in that Jameson is with her and give him a nod. We weren't close friends in school – or since – his allegiance always very clearly with Kade and Camilla and the trio they make. But we never had animosity either. Plus, he's friends with my friends – not as close as me, but still.

Kade's laugh comes again, a sound so natural and enveloping it coats my skin in goosebumps. A sound I haven't heard from him much. But I guess I haven't often given him reason to.

'I didn't know you were coming,' he says, accepting Camilla's embrace with the arm not holding Nightshade.

I gently take the reins from him and glance around at this family celebration I don't need to be part of. Although it doesn't escape my attention that his sister is, in fact, here and very clearly in support. Perhaps Kade's not the only one with a complicated relationship with their grandfather.

'I'll get him set. You ... do this,' I murmur, gesturing between him and Camilla.

Kade looks between me and the others. 'You staying?' he asks them. 'You'll have a drink with us?'

I catch the quirk of Camilla's mouth before I turn away and walk Nightshade – faster than is really necessary – away from Kade Wilder, who just referred to us as ... *us*.

Nightshade's stable is mucked out and he's happily snuffling through the flake of hay I've popped in his feeding net by the time I've finished brushing him down and ferrying all his gear back and forth to the small tack room in Kade's gooseneck.

'Evening, Ms Archer.'

The voice is deep as it cuts across the run of stables that now feel eerily quiet around me.

Suppressing the shiver that prickles the back of my neck, I turn to find Kade's grandfather waiting for me.

'Evening,' I say tightly, sliding the bridle off the top rung of the stable wall and moving to walk past. Whatever he's doing here isn't going to be good. What would my grandfather think of me having to come face to face with Walter Wilder on my own, in the near dark, with—

'Interesting run you had today,' he remarks, stepping into my path.

My blood cools. His presence alone sets my nerves on edge, like he could snap at any moment. But I can't downplay either Nightshade or Kade. I glance over my shoulder, realising I can't leave until he has – I don't trust him with my horse. Not after what he did to some of our previous champions. Time may have moved on since then, but I haven't.

I take a step back towards the stable and he smiles.

'That's an impressive beast you've got,' he says, and I remain silent. 'I can see why you'd like to further his bloodline.' He takes another step forward, any semblance of a smile vanishing from his face. 'Mark my words, girly – you run him again with a Wilder and your stud will be over before it's even started. And if I find you've tried to seduce my grandson – even if he's a fucking disgrace of a Wilder – I'll rip that poor excuse of a station from you just because I can.'

He turns on his heel and walks away, my heart pounding harder with every step.

We've been sitting around a small camp table for the last thirty minutes and I still can't seem to steady the pace of my pulse. Every time I think I might finally be able to breathe and have as normal a conversation as possible with three people I've actively avoided my whole life – particularly after my interaction with Walter Wilder – some part of Kade brushes against me.

His knuckles when we reach into the chip bowl at the same time, his thigh when he shifts on the hard bench seat, his elbow as he smooths a hand down his chest – an action I try really hard not to follow with my gaze.

Their rhythm strikes me as so similar to mine with Marlowe, Linden, and Juniper, and it makes me miss my friends. At the same time ... it's almost verging on comforting after seeing Kade's grandfather. Not something I'd ever have dreamed of saying about spending time with the Wilder siblings and the man who may as well be a Wilder.

Camilla laughs, half choking on the mouthful of beer she just took. 'I did not!'

Kade raises his brows at her, a smirk forming. 'Oh, my mistake, it was my other sister. The one who knows how to reverse a truck and not take out the carport.'

Jameson chuckles quietly and Camilla gasps at him. 'You did not just take his side!'

'Cami, sweetheart, it took me half a day to fix that support post before your grandfather noticed, and I nearly killed myself in the process. It was definitely you,' Jameson replies, a half-smile on his face as if he wouldn't have had it any other way.

She blushes and rolls her eyes. 'Fine, I concede.'

Kade laughs out loud, and I can't help the tug at the corner of my mouth the sound creates. 'I love that you really thought we had no idea it was you.' He shakes his head and looks at me. 'Did you ever wish for siblings?' he asks, and the question makes me pause.

'Once. Then I met Linden and Juniper, and then Marlowe, and they became so much more than just my friends. They're the brother and sisters I chose.'

'I don't know how you don't just turn into a complete fangirl around Juniper,' Camilla says with a smile, a strand of blonde hair drifting across her face in the breeze.

I twist the stem of my plastic wine glass between my fingers. 'It's hard to fangirl over someone I've watched drool into their pillow on more than one occasion. But do *not* tell her I told you that.'

Camilla throws her head back and laughs, and I can't help but join in, feeling Kade's attention settle on me as I do. Under the table, his knee presses gently into mine and my stomach flips.

'Okay,' Jameson declares as proper dark begins to fall. 'It's time we head out so I can check on the bar before close.' He holds out a hand to Camilla to help her off the bench, and we say our goodbyes, my chest feeling a little warmer after spending the evening with them.

'Oh.' Jameson pauses in his walk towards his truck and looks back. 'Do you need an extra swag?'

I could swear there's a twinkle in his eyes despite the distance.

'Nah, we're good,' Kade answers.

We stand in silence as we watch Jameson and Camilla climb into the truck and drive away. They've got a few hours ahead of them to get back to Blackwood Valley and then bar work, so I imagine they'll be exhausted tomorrow.

As the red tail lights disappear around the run of arenas that sit in the middle of Wentworth Station's camping spots, the darkening blue sky presses in on me. I bite my bottom lip as my skin begins to prickle. Kade's presence is like a living thing next to me, as though I could turn to him and run my fingers through the richness of the air between us. I suppress a shiver.

'Cold?' he asks, looking down at me over his shoulder. 'I've got an extra blanket under the bed.'

'Ah,' I mumble, unable to stop the physical memory of waking up virtually wrapped in Kade – one that makes me warm enough. 'No, I'm okay, thank you.'

'I'll wash the dishes,' he says, giving me a long look before turning back to camp.

I grab the tea towel resting on the camping table and wordlessly start drying what Kade hands me, our fingers catching through the fabric every now and then. A sensation I try not to seek out.

'You're very quiet over there,' he remarks, focusing on his hands in the soapy water. 'You okay?'

Swallowing, I wonder how much to tell him about my visit with Walter. It's so clear now that they're nothing alike but ...

'I just ... I saw your grandfather in the stables.'

Kade pauses before turning slowly to face me. 'And?'

I let my gaze run over him as I consider my response. Does Kade know how openly his grandfather shares his disdain for him? 'He made his position clear on you riding Nightshade.'

His navy gaze – almost black in the low light – surveys me, as though he knows that can't be all of it, and my chest pinches with the need to erase the worry from his features. I gently brush the back of his arm.

'I'm good. It's fine.'

He makes a doubtful sound in the back of his throat but eventually returns his attention to the dishes. I listen to the noises drifting over from other competitors settling in for the night.

'So are you also reeling from the fact that you've spent time with another Wilder who doesn't have devil horns?' Kade asks after long moments of silence.

The smile on his face draws a laugh from me as I give him a sideways glance and push away all thought of his grandfather – what he said wasn't anything I hadn't expected – and the more time I spend with Kade and Camilla, the clearer it becomes that neither of them are anything like him.

'I haven't decided you don't yet either,' I say.

Before I can register the gleam in his eyes, he flicks me with soapy bubbles. 'Maybe you just haven't looked hard enough.'

Chapter Seventeen

KADE

Spending another night with Temperance and not knowing if she wants me to touch her or not has me in more knots than I would have expected. On one hand, I feel her looking at me more often than not, and I can *see* a want in her face that definitely wasn't there before. At least, not before that night in my storeroom. The night I think about way more than I should.

The night something shifted irreversibly.

And yet, I also see her glance away when I catch her looking. Or when she catches me in a daze as I watch how the roundness of her cheeks creeps higher when she tries not to smile at me. Or how she bites the inside of her bottom lip when we hold eye contact for a little too long.

But I shouldn't even want to touch her, should I? The woman who has made no secret of her hate for my family for as long as I can remember.

So why does the sight of her in an oversized top and pants that have clearly seen a lot of nights in her swag make my dick take note? And that's not even mentioning how she looks crawling over the end of my bed towards her pillow.

I swallow as my cock hardens in my shorts.

Fuck.

I force myself to stare at the dark ceiling and bite the inside of my cheek as she settles in beside me.

'Nervous?' she asks, and I close my eyes for a moment. 'For tomorrow's ride?'

No, not what I was thinking – but I'll take the out. Or let her have it. Either way, it's a distraction from imagining her crawling towards me without those fucking clothes.

I can feel her soft breath on my shoulder and know she's facing me, so I roll over as well, letting my top arm drape across my chest, my palm down on the mattress between us. How easy it would be to reach out and brush her cheek with my fingers. See if it's still as soft as it looks.

'Yeah, a little,' I say quietly, wondering if she knows there's more behind the words. Tomorrow, the next day, the day after that ... I don't know when – or if – it will break, but something is shifting under our feet here. Something that feels a lot more dangerous than just riding her horse.

She holds my gaze as she laces her fingers between mine, our hands now joined between us, and I hope like hell she can't hear how loud my heart is racing.

'Tonight was ... nice,' she whispers.

And we fall asleep like that, silently watching each other in the soft glow of the interior night lights. Hands clasped like there's nothing more natural in the world.

Reined cow horse is my favourite event. I like the precision and technique in the reining, but it's hard to beat the way the world fades away when a horse and I home in on a cow and I give myself over to the horse and their instincts.

I set it up, move us around the pen, and choose the beast to isolate. But there's a moment – sometimes it's a slow build of understanding and, other times, it's faster than a blink. A moment where the horse and I become a single mind, and it's more about me moving with the horse than telling them what to do. Somewhere along the way in their training, they just ... get it.

Nightshade has that instinct in spades. So, as I ride him out of the arena, I know he's the one who's got us a qualifying score – one that will have every reiner and breeder within a hundred miles looking a little more closely at Temperance Archer and what she's building with her stud.

Packing up in the afternoon sun as quickly as we can, we spend the drive home reliving every moment of the runs and the conversations we had that were promising for future servicing requests for Nightshade.

'I hope you're proud,' she announces suddenly, and my heart skips. The words are missing the bite my grandfather used to use them with, but I've rarely heard them without a sting in the tail. Or a busted lip.

'Of what?' I ask carefully, my voice a shade too low.

I glance at her in the passenger seat and catch her frowning a little at me. Please let that be confusion and not disgust.

'Kade,' she says firmly. 'You just smashed the hell out of that event. You backed yourself, convinced me – your enemy, if you recall – to pair you with my best horse, and you just … rode out there and did the thing. We got qualifying scores! Two more events like that and we go to Nationals.'

I don't know what to say to that. My mind is caught reeling by the fact that she doesn't sound pissed. She sounds … *pleased*? With me? And in the same breath, she called herself my enemy. She can't honestly believe that after this weekend. Surely.

She shifts in her seat so she's facing me more fully, and I focus on the road ahead – the tall pines lining one side as a windbreak for the farm that stretches for miles back the way we've come.

'You can't say it, can you?' she asks, serious now.

I run my hand through my hair and squeeze the back of my neck. How do I tell her the last time I was asked if I felt proud was after I'd paid for Cami's first year at uni – as much as I could afford. My grandfather had expressly told me she wasn't to go. He didn't tell her that, of course. That was supposed to be my job – crush her dreams. But I paid, sent her away to chase them.

He got out his belt.

He didn't use it that time. But the action was reminder enough of what he can – and would – do. And what I'd be forced to take.

'Kade?' she murmurs, pulling me out of the memory. 'I'm going to take that as an affirmative – you can't say it.' She clears her throat, and I wrap my hands tighter around the steering wheel, scrambling for another direction to take the conversation.

'Okay.' I see her nod in my periphery. 'Well, *I'm* proud of you. Perhaps that doesn't mean a lot coming from an Archer, but I am. And ... I'm proud of me for not marching you off my property that day when I *very* desperately wanted to.'

The laugh that escapes me surprises us both.

'Okay?' she asks.

I smile out the window. 'Okay.'

The silence for the rest of the drive is comfortable. Warm, even, and I find myself glancing at her every few minutes, taking in what I can of her profile before turning my attention back to the road. I'm both disappointed the hours-long trip is ending and full of nervous energy as I turn left onto her drive.

Temperance draws a deep breath and stretches as we approach the round yard, outside of which we'll unload Nightshade before brushing him down and feeding him, ready to turn out for the night.

The sound she makes as she lifts her arms overhead hits me right in the groin, and I force myself not to look at her. Not to see if any sliver of skin peeks out beneath her red shirt before she drops her arms.

Once the stallion is looked after, and we've agreed he'll have three days' rest before I come back to work him again, we stand watching each other in the dying light. The sunset over her farm, beyond the river, ignites the sky in a deep orange that sets her – and her hair – at the centre of a flame.

'I guess that's the weekend done, then,' I make myself say.

She nods. 'Yup. Have a good night. See you in a few.'

She turns and starts towards the house, unaware, I hope, that I'm soaking in the view of her round ass as she goes. I bet it would feel good to squeeze. Bite.

Fuck, I need to leave.

I wait until she reaches the door. She looks back, and my mouth goes dry. But she says nothing, then disappears inside.

Forcing myself into my truck, I press my head against the headrest. Logically, I know I should leave. But after spending the last two nights in the same bed, there's a physical tether now. Like I couldn't drive away even if I tried. Like we're not done tonight.

Hoping I'm not making a very embarrassing decision, I reach into the back for my bag, dig out the bottle, and send her a photo.

Chapter Eighteen

TEMPERANCE

Kade's truck is still sitting outside my round yard, clearly visible from my kitchen window. I know he's in there – I heard the door close – but he hasn't gone anywhere, and I have the craziest thought that I should invite him in.

I shove it aside as my phone vibrates on the bench.

What I need with Kade Wilder is distance. Distance, distance, distance. No more bed sharing, wet swag or not – his warm, hard body has muddled my senses. Not to mention how he looks in a pair of jeans.

Damn it. Distance is the last thing I want.

Dragging a hand down my face, I pick up my phone. My heart rate spikes when I see it's Kade messaging me. From outside.

It's a picture of a bottle of gin. One that looks suspiciously like the one he wouldn't let me take from his storeroom.

And a question mark.

I immediately break out into a sweat. Sharing that bed was one thing.

Then I held his hand and watched him fall asleep.

Told him I was proud of him.

And his grandfather said he'd ruin me.

My throat thickens and my mind wanders to the breadth of Kade's shoulders as he lay breathing calmly beside me. How he strode towards me like I was the only thing in his world when he came off that arena. How he's been nothing but an exceptional gentleman – and very, very different to Walter. There's a flutter between my legs I know I should ignore. But when I couple it with the ache in my chest at the thought of him driving away, I open the cupboard and send him a photo back.

Two glasses on my bench.

A moment later his truck door closes again, and I race to the bathroom.

Oh god. I look like a complete mess. My hair has escaped my braid so much it's more lion's mane than braid, my face is streaked with dirt, and I've got mascara under my—

There's a knock at the kitchen door – the same door I locked him out of not long ago – and a kaleidoscope of butterflies erupts in my gut. What the fuck am I doing?

And yet, my body is all too keen to answer the door, lion's mane be damned.

The man who fills my doorway makes my knees wobble.

'Hey,' he murmurs, his voice low, sliding along my collarbones. His navy eyes drink me in, taking in every flushed inch of my face. 'Thought it was as good a time as any for you to try my best.' He holds the bottle out as I raise a brow.

'Your best?'

'Well,' he says, a grin spreading slow and confident, 'my best *gin*. We can save my other bests for another time.'

Then he winks, and my stomach flips over itself.

I can't help but smile back.

'What if I've already had the best?'

His eyes sparkle. He leans in, close enough our noses might touch if I tilt forward even a fraction. 'Impossible.'

My gaze drops to his chest, and I force myself to breathe. It's a mistake. All I inhale is Kade – dust, sweat, horses, and something warm and woodsy beneath it. My eyes flutter shut and I pinch my side, clawing back some semblance of sense.

Stepping aside, I let him in.

'Over to you,' I offer, gesturing to the glasses on the bench.

I take a seat on a barstool and watch him on the other side, trying not to notice how natural he seems in my kitchen – washing his hands, finding the glasses, preparing our drinks. He slides one towards me.

'Try it neat first,' he suggests.

Drawing in a deep inhale – not unlike the breath I took of *him* – I'm surrounded by the feeling of summer. Riding through meadows of wildflowers. Picnics at sunset. I'm hopeless at identifying individual flavours, but this gin summons all of it.

'It's ... romantic,' I say, realising too late what I've just blurted.

He runs a thumb over his lip, and I watch the movement. *Fuck.*

'I don't disagree. It's my favourite limited edition so far.' He plants both hands on the bench, squaring off at me. 'Might stay that way too.'

I swallow. The way he's looking at me makes me feel drunker than I was that night in his bar. And I certainly wasn't drunk enough then to forget how it felt to be held against him. *That's okay*, I tell myself. I'll just keep on this side of the island bench. It's just one drink, and then he has to drive.

'What do you use to make the flavours?' I ask.

He blinks, as if I've pulled him from a runaway thought.

'Botanicals. But I try to source locally where I can, which can be limiting – there's not a lot of growers out here. Anyone working the land is mostly a farmer.'

I stare at him, weighing up whether he's being cagey or if he genuinely has no idea how large my fields are.

'You ... haven't ventured around the other side of the house?' He's been here plenty of times without me watching his every move; I just sort of assumed he'd have scoped out what he could. Even if I *have* kept my mares and other stallion in the far paddocks.

'I wasn't invited to. What's there?'

I take a sip of the summertime gin he's poured for me and let the flavours roll over my tongue.

'Hmm, this is good. And my flower farm. I provide for the wedding crowd mostly, and some markets, as you know. But ... it's building.'

His lips part slightly.

'When, exactly, do you have time to run this stud and care for a flower farm that can accommodate the weddings that happen here? I thought you just did the markets. And Doris's.'

I laugh and take another sip. 'Apparently I think sleep is overrated.'

I try to make it sound light, but I know I've failed when he tilts his head, thick brows pulling together.

Sighing, I decide I may as well confirm what he must already suspect.

'The stud is barely functioning – hence my need to get Nightshade on the circuit – and in case you haven't noticed, things aren't quite in tip-top shape around here. Not like the Wilder Station I imagine. I had to find an alternative income stream. Plus, I do virtual data entry sometimes, which is ... kind of mind-numbing. But the flower business is doing well. Just takes a huge amount of work.'

He blows out a breath and runs a hand down his short beard.

'You know, it's kind of intimidating how hard you're working to get this all going again.'

I laugh and take another sip, my mouth warming.

'That's not what I expected you to say.'

'And what was, then?'

I sit back a little. 'I don't know ... maybe some sort of half-apology for something we both know had nothing to do with you. Or, worse, an explanation of why it was okay my grandfather got screwed over.'

He makes a sound in the back of his throat and drains his drink, lifting the bottle in a question.

I finish mine and push my glass towards him.

'Right,' he says, grabbing the second bottle he brought in, 'this time with tonic.'

I watch as he finds ice in my freezer and pours us each another drink, but my heart starts to hammer when he comes around to my side of the counter and takes the barstool next to me.

He turns so he's fully facing me, and my body involuntarily mirrors him. Like he's a fucking magnet my cells are attuned to.

'Temperance – for the record – I will never think it's okay for someone to screw you over.'

I stare at him, taking in the full, beard-lined lips that just said words still vibrating under my ribs, sending a tingle down my limbs. His trim beard practically begs me to slide my fingers into it, to find the warmth of his skin beneath, to trace the shape of his jaw.

'You really mean that, don't you?' I ask.

He reaches between my legs and drags my stool closer until my thighs are pressed between his – knees braced against his stool and so close to the bulge in his pants I forget how to breathe.

'Yes, I fucking mean it, Temperance. I might be a lot of things, but I'm not someone who delights in others' misfortune – planned or otherwise – or in their pain.'

He watches me for a long moment, his gaze softening, almost begging me to see – *to feel* – what he's saying.

'I'm really not.'

But the truth is, I already know that. And if I'm honest, I've known it since school. Since I watched him look after Camilla and forge a friendship with her and Jameson that left me envious – at least until I found my own people. It was obvious Camilla would always side with him, but the way she idolised him, and Jamie supported him, gave me pause. A pause I didn't want to acknowledge at the time – not when my grandfather had just lost everything, his health was declining, and my legacy was in shambles.

I cup his face in my palm, the heat of his skin making me blink. Part of me is surprised I've done it; the other part is certain I'll never *not* be drawn to touch him. Not when he's sitting so close, his body angled towards mine like I'm some kind of gravitational centre. And certainly not while his dark blue eyes search me with an intensity that makes my skin prickle.

Slowly, he lifts his hand and places it over mine, sliding his fingers around the back. Keeping his gaze locked on mine, he drags my hand over his face, his beard scratching against my skin in a way that makes my pussy throb, and presses an open-mouthed kiss to my palm.

Chapter Nineteen

KADE

Temperance's breath hitches as she watches me place kisses up the inside of her wrist and along the underside of her forearm, up to where her shirt sleeve is rolled. I don't let go of the back of her hand as I guide it away from her body and along my mouth. Her eyelids start to droop, and I lick the inside of her wrist again because I can't get enough of how she tastes. How she feels against my tongue.

My cock hardens fast as I think about where else I'd like to lick her.

Swallowing, I lower her hand to her thigh, resting mine on top of it. She can either pull me closer or push me away from here. The next move is hers.

Having her here – literally between my legs – is making my pulse roar so loudly I can barely think. But the last two nights we've been toeing a very obvious line, and now I've just demolished it. I need to know it's not just me going out on a huge fucking limb here. Need to know she's been learning as much about me as I have about her – knowledge burrowing into places so deep I'm not sure I'll ever be able to remove it.

I watch her chest rise and fall, her perfect tits lifting under her shirt. A shirt I desperately want to tear open just to get a look at them, see how they'd move under my hands. My fingers tighten on her thigh, and I drag in air like it might help make sense of what we're doing. As if it could calm the almost painful way my jeans are digging into my hard-on.

A small groan escapes her, and I rake a hand through my hair and squeeze the back of my neck, grounding myself.

Gently, she pulls her hand from under mine – and my stomach sinks.

Until she reverses the grip and guides my hand up her thigh, right towards her pussy.

Oh fuck. She's really doing that.

Her jeans are warm and worn, and the shape of her fits perfectly against my palm. I drag my thumb over the seam running over her and apply a small amount of pressure. Her jade eyes glaze as she draws a slow, deep inhale that makes my dick kick in my pants.

I do it again – firmer this time – and she presses back against my hand, showing me exactly how much pressure she wants as I rub the seam against her. Her hips rock slowly, gently, but enough for me to know she wants more. Is *asking* for more. She whimpers softly when I take my thumb away, and her eyes widen as she watches me undo the button of her jeans.

Temperance bites her lip, gaze flicking up to mine. She lifts her hips, and I slide her jeans down, wriggling them along her pale thighs and over her knees. I watch every inch I uncover: the soft skin, the pale scar on her left knee. When her jeans hit the floor, I peel off her thick, dusty work socks, exposing delicate feet with bright red nail polish. Only then do I let my gaze travel back up to her pussy, hidden behind plain purple panties. My cock hardens further, desperate against the denim, but this isn't about me. It's about what she's willing to give. How far she's willing to take this.

How much of herself she's willing to give to me.

I grip the underside of her thighs and pull her legs out from between mine, draping them over my lap and forcing her to lean back, bracing on the stool's low back as I drag her even closer.

'You're fucking gorgeous,' I breathe, taking in her spread thighs, her skin against my jeans, how unabashedly she exposes herself to me.

The darkening patch on her panties tells me exactly how wet she is for me.

Sliding a hand up each thigh, I follow the imprint my fingers make – the way her soft flesh yields beneath my palms – and I wonder what it would be like to bite her ass. To grab it and pull her back onto me as I bury myself deep within her.

But that's not for now.

Now, I clear my throat, firmly instructing my cock not to blow in my fucking pants because, tonight, I'm going to make sure Temperance Archer remembers none of the reasons she didn't want to be associated with me. Show her she made a good decision letting me this close to her life. Because I have a sinking suspicion I'm not going to want to leave it.

She gasps as I grip her hips and hook a thumb under each side of her underwear, stroking the outside of her cunt. Finding where satin-soft skin meets a small patch of hair. I slide my right thumb along her slit, grinning at the wetness I find. She huffs a small smile until I work my way down to her entrance, circling it before dragging her arousal back up over her clit. Her head falls back, mouth open towards the ceiling as she curses and rocks harder into me.

'Please, Kade,' she whispers, unlocking a kink I didn't know I had – Temperance Archer, spread and begging, murmuring my name.

I let her sit in that need for a beat while I tease her, knowing full well it isn't enough to take her over the edge yet. Then I tug her panties down slightly, taking my fill as I drink her in.

'Please what, Sundance?' I murmur. 'It's such a pretty cunt ... you're not really trying to hurry me, are you?'

The groan that rumbles in her chest is like my personal aphrodisiac. I shift in my seat and take a deep breath as Temperance presses into my hands again.

'Make me come, Kade. I want to—'

She cries out when I slip my thumb into her, as deep as it will go, her pussy flexing around me. Shifting my left hand from her hip, I drag down the front of her panties so they're tight across the tops of her thighs, digging into her sides, and circle her clit with two fingers. A hypnotising pink flush creeps up her neck. Her breaths go ragged, the rhythm of her rocking steady. Needy. She white-knuckles the edge of her seat when I replace my thumb with a finger, pressing deep and pulsing into the slick heat of her.

'More,' she breathes. 'More.'

She doesn't need to ask twice. I shove two more fingers into her, picking up the pace with each hand so they match in speed and pressure. Her pussy squeezes around me, and I give her just a little more – fingers pumping inside her as I press down on her clit and circle hard with the other hand. The desperation in her moans, and that she hasn't backed off once, tells me she does *not* want gentle right now. Her thighs tighten, legs starting to pull together, muscles trembling. The flush crawls along her jawline, and my fingers are soaked with her need.

Her mouth drops open like she's going to speak, but her eyes fall closed and the sound that tears from her reverberates through my bones. Her cunt grasps at my fingers as I coax her pleasure out for as long as I can.

And then I hold her there, cupping her most intimate place until the shaking subsides and she slowly blinks her dazed eyes open. There's something precarious in this – temporary, maybe – but as I watch her, something in me shifts in a way I'm not sure I'll ever undo.

Carefully, she sits up. I let my hands slide out and retreat to her thighs, running my short nails across her skin, watching the bumps rise and her gaze sharpen back on me.

A grin kicks up on one side of her mouth.

'That's some fucking gin.'

Chapter Twenty

TEMPERANCE

Three days. That's how long it will be before I see Kade again, and I can't work out if that's a fantastic blessing or the longest wait I'll ever have to endure. I could barely walk to see him out of my house after we drank our last gin with me pantless – legs crossed between his as he lazily trailed his fingers over my thighs and sent my brain cells scattering.

I almost asked him to stay.

Almost leaned forward and kissed him.

Oh god, imagine if I'd kissed him?

I can't deny there's a very insistent part of me that wanted to do exactly that. Feel what his pale pink lips would be like against mine. Would he bite me? Lick the corner of my mouth? Suck my tongue? How often could we do it? But his grand—

'What's got you all dreamy-looking?' Marlowe asks as she lowers herself into a chair on my right.

My heart leaps in my chest; I didn't even hear her arrive. Not that I've noticed much about what's happening in the café around me as I try not to look at Kade's bar across the road.

Marlowe drops her bag and peers at me.

'Trust me,' Linden says, folding himself heavily into the chair on my other side, 'she's not going to have as many wrinkles as I do, you can stop looking.'

'No,' Marlowe muses distractedly. 'It's something else.'

I pick up the specials menu. 'Just running through the pattern for the next qualifier.'

Linden laughs, looking at Marlowe as if I'm not sitting right between them. 'You're right, there's something else. Could it be ...' He studies me, then his mouth drops open. 'No! You're not daydreaming about your *rider*, are you? There's only one thing that could give you that face and that's—'

'Seriously, Lin,' Marlowe cuts in, picking up her own menu. 'She'd rather kill that man than consider he's actually one of the valley's most eligible bachelors for a reason.'

I press my lips together, and she slowly lowers the brown paper she's holding, pinning me with her dark, knowing gaze.

'You haven't flown off the handle in a fit of outraged denial yet, *Temperance*.'

Dropping my head into my hands, I press my palms to my eyes as if I could hide from this conversation. Hide from the reality of what Kade is clearly not ... and how wrong I've been about him for so long. Hide from what Walter Wilder would do to me if he ever found out.

'Holy shit,' Linden remarks, then glances at the waitress who appears beside us. 'Oh, I'll have the granola, and she'll have ... let's say ricotta pancakes.'

Marlowe orders fruit salad with a side of hash browns and bacon, the waitress murmurs something, and leaves.

'Well,' Linden says, settling back, 'this is an interesting turn of events.'

'I knew I wasn't so drunk I made up the fact that you were pressed against him at the bar!'

I look at Marlowe as Linden stares between us. 'The night Junie was here? Exactly why did no one tell me this?'

'Ugh,' I mutter. 'Okay. I have a big fucking problem.'

They both stare at me as if they can't imagine what could possibly come next.

'You're right, Kade isn't all bad ...'

I can feel the smile creep across my face as they hoot with laughter.

'Well,' Linden drawls, smiling gratefully at the waitress as she brings his coffee, 'I'm a little dumbfounded. But that's a pretty wicked smile you're rocking right now. Even if you *are* crushing on your biggest fucking enemy.' He sighs, looking between us. 'At least one of us is doing something exciting. I think I'm failing at everything.'

'I think being a new single dad gives you an out, Lin,' I say gently. He's hard enough on himself about his sister's death, this is hardly something to add to the list of ways he thinks he's failing. 'And Coco adores you. You're giving her a village.' I think of how she ran to Kade, a warmth settling over me. 'That's pretty special.'

He purses his lips. 'Yeah, maybe. She did love hanging out with Juniper that weekend too. But she doesn't see her enough, and every time she does, there's just another goodbye looming around the corner.'

I let that settle, unsure how to make him feel better about the fact that his best friend is almost never here – off living the musician's dream he could have had too.

Marlowe reaches out and squeezes his forearm as he runs a hand through his hair. 'Anyway, talk to me more about Kade. And you, Lowe, how's Henry?'

Marlowe's brows pinch as she takes her food from the waitress. 'It's fine, I guess – he's fine. Good. We're going away for the weekend soon, which will be nice.'

'That's great,' I reply. 'You need to let your hair down. Have some fun with your boyfriend.'

'Oh right, says the one who hadn't even looked at a man in years until a tall, bearded blond offered to ride—'

'Do *not* finish that sentence,' I cut in, sitting back as the waitress – one I don't recognise and who is probably here for some holiday work – slides my plate of pancakes onto the table.

Linden clears his throat and the mood drops. 'Seriously though, Peri, is this a good idea?'

All the reasons why it was a terrible idea to even let him onto my property hit me square in the chest.

'Honestly, no. His grandfather has already – very clearly – told me if Kade rode again he'd make sure my stud was discredited before it even started.'

The look they each give me is one of horror – for me, I can tell, but also for what that means for Kade and how Walter views him. It makes my bones feel weary.

'He also said ... if I tried to seduce a Wilder – which I have *not*, this has been ... surprising for me too – but if I seduced even, I quote, "a disgrace" of a Wilder, he'd take everything from me.'

Marlowe sits back, a delicate frown between her brows. 'Wow, that's unbelievable. What a horrible man. But he can't do that.'

'Yes, actually, he can,' I say. 'He might be in the older generation of the horse circuits, but he has more connections than I could ever dream of. All it would take is one person to believe whatever he might say and it could be such an uphill battle – more so even than now – that I could just never get the stud off the ground.'

Linden places a hand on my forearm. 'Listen, I actually quite like the guy – Kade – have since school, but was never brave enough to tell you. And I never liked him more than you anyway, so all good. But nice guy or not, is the risk worth it? Walter is not only connected, like you said, he's head of one of the most powerful livestock boards in this region, *and* he's on the local council.'

Marlowe frowns at him, her dark brows drawing low over her equally dark lashes. 'What's livestock got to do with Peri – she doesn't have any?'

Linden shakes his head but keeps his gaze on me. 'No – but here, that doesn't matter. Most people do, and the traditional ways run hard. One sentence from Walter and her whole business – both flowers and stud – won't stand a chance.'

'You're right,' I admit after a moment, and they both look at me with a shadow of concern.

'It's more than "Kade's not all bad", isn't it?' Marlowe asks, examining me like I imagine she might examine a client she's trying to see through. 'We know you, Peri – there's no way you've let your feelings wander there just for fun or to … you know.'

'Nope,' I say, too quickly.

A sinking feeling fills me at what that means, and at the knowledge that if Walter Wilder was prepared to so blatantly threaten me, what he's prepared to do to Kade for associating with me is likely far, far worse.

Linden squeezes my arm as his phone chimes. 'Listen,' he begins, still glancing at his phone. 'I know I just asked if it's worth it, but I'm changing my mind – why should that old man get to decide what is and isn't yours? But I do think you need to be careful. If you think this thing with Kade could be serious, then you need to fight for it. If it's not, then maybe let it go.'

He tucks into his breakfast and, mercifully, moves us on to talking about the latest thing his niece Coco has been doing. But it takes me longer than I'd like to admit to catch up to the conversation and not feel like I'm scrambling. Because the thought of not being that close to Kade again doesn't just make me think of the mind-blowing climax he gave me – it makes something in my chest pinch.

And it hurts.

Chapter Twenty-One

KADE

I can't wipe the fucking smile off my face. I wish I could say it was annoying, but the memory of Temperance – her luscious thighs spread just for me – is one I'm going to enjoy for a very long time.

Slightly less convenient is the way Jamie and Cami keep side-eyeing me.

Having left her place late last night, against everything in me screaming to stay – and not only my rock-hard cock – I was up early again this morning to work the Wilder horses. As I brush down Pix, I push away the sharp pang that I won't be able to do this much longer.

He gave me that one ride. What he doesn't know is that I have no intention of stopping there. I love these horses, and I'll give them everything of me for as long as I can. But they're Brody's and Tray's to ride.

Nightshade is mine.

So is my relationship – whatever that may be – with Temperance.

And I don't intend to let either of them down.

We're supposed to be resting Nightshade for a couple more days, but my skin is itching to see Temperance again.

149

There's a small part of me gnawing on the possibility she's mortified. But I have to know.

The knowledge of how soft her skin is ... how wet she was for me ... the way her underwear tightened like a strap around the top of her thighs ...

All of that may have been enough for me to fist myself to release on my shower wall several times over, but there's a deep gnawing in my gut that it will never be enough now.

Meadow and Velvet is quiet when I get in, its daily activity not yet started, but Jamie – and probably Cami too – won't be far away. She might only be here on her summer break, but she's hustling hard for me to see her as a key, and likely permanent, fixture of Meadow and Velvet.

I don't tell her that's a future I'd love her to have too. She needs more options than that, and her degree will give them to her. Hopefully, after she gets the degree she's promised me, she'll find a life so bright and sparkling she'll never want to come back.

I finish the count of the gin I'm supposed to be doing in the storeroom and try – unsuccessfully – to push away the memory of Temperance in this room too. The moment that seemed to start it all. But it's more than the memory occupying all the space in my mind. It's the truth that it's not just her wanting body that's going to haunt me. It's the deep ache in my chest she's opened up – the need to be near her. By giving me that secret smile she thinks I don't notice when I say something amusing or when I'm working with her horse. By the way she actively wants to calm my nerves and support me in a way I haven't let any other woman.

What is it about her that's left me wide open?

Jamie and Cami are suspiciously quiet when I leave the storeroom and find them in the main bar, which is fine by me. I don't want to share anything about last night with them. Not yet. Not when it's possible Temperance is sick with regret this morning. My gut swirls. I need to know where she's at.

Is this – us – dominating her every thought the way it is mine?

'Still riding your high?' Jamie asks from across the space, as he places lunch menus on the tables.

I can't help but laugh. 'Yep.'

Cami follows behind him with a small vase of flowers that are clearly meant for decoration, and I raise a brow. 'It's good for the vibe,' she says, shrugging one shoulder.

I survey the bar. The warm, rustic wood with its slightly industrial lights and flowers. It almost looks ... like other events could happen here. Something Cami has been at me to consider for a while. But I can't take that on right now, and Jamie already has to bust his ass in the kitchen, leading the team in there and covering for me while I work on the station. I wonder if I could entice Beckett to stay here for a bit? He's officially out of the military now and contracting as a builder, which means he can be flexible.

My gaze drifts back to the flowers, and I think about Temperance's admission about her farm. I snap a photo of the bunch.

As good as yours? I type, sending the photo to her.

I pocket my phone quickly and try to force myself into some state of patience, and not immediately obsessing over whether she'll respond.

'Kade?' Cami asks, and I glance up to find her and Jamie staring at me.

'Sorry, I was just thinking about Beckett. He's just left his last contract and is kind of between things. He could be good in the kitchen to free you up a bit, Jamie?'

Cami raises her brows as Jamie flicks her a look I can't read, before turning back to me.

'You want your cousin back here to free me up?' he asks, looking at Cami again. This time I don't miss the anticipation in her expression – as if 'freeing Jamie up' is the answer to some hope I haven't been clued in on.

'What have you two been planning?'

'Not much,' Jamie replies, and I can't help but laugh.

'Jamie, my friend,' I say. 'You and I both know the dreams you two could concoct if you wanted. But no – I was thinking more like giving you some head space to live a little. Maybe be a bit more strategic with Meadow and Velvet *without* Cami.'

She groans and turns away, busying herself with the rest of the flowers. 'Well, I think it's a great idea. The country air will be good for Beckett, and it'll give the three of us some space to work out what comes next. I *will* be part of this bar sooner or later, big brother.'

'Got to admire her tenacity,' Jamie remarks, one corner of his mustache kicked up in a crooked smile.

A sinking feeling coats my stomach. 'Cami, you're what – three assessments away from finishing your degree? Then you can teach *wherever* you want.'

'Correct, Kade. I can go *wherever* I want.'

I shake my head. 'No. Blackwood Valley is out for you, and you know it is. You don't want to teach here anyway – you said so yourself. Not to mention, you *promised* me you'd finish. I – we – will miss you something fierce, but you deserve more than our bar, Cami.'

The room falls silent for a moment, and I can tell she's winding up for her counter-argument. The truth is, I'd love to have her here. It goes against every fibre to send her away again; the relief I felt when she came home for her break was palpable.

But it doesn't change that it will be much, much better for her to stay the hell away from our grandfather. I've poked that bear enough for the two of us.

'He's right,' Jamie admits, and something in her face falls so hard I feel it in my chest. She stares at Jamie for so long I start to wonder what the fuck I'm missing.

She sighs. 'Yes, okay. He's right. Three more assessments and then I'll be moving to the city for a beginner teacher role.'

'Good for you,' Jamie says, although it sounds as strangled as I feel.

I try to smile at her, but it comes out more of a grimace.

'But mark my words, both of you,' she declares, pointing at each of us. 'I try it your way and it doesn't work out, I *will* do whatever the hell I please and neither of you will say a damn thing, got it?'

I exchange a look with Jamie, surprised at the sudden strength of her statement, but I know she means it.

'I get it, Cami, I really do. I just ...' I take a step towards her and sigh. 'I just don't want him to be able to claim your success as his own. Or dig his hooks into you in any way.'

I don't tell her that I've happily played buffer between him and her for her whole life, and the more I'm cut out of it, the more risk I think she's in. I know the fear and anger that simmers under the surface – bone-deep, soul-rattling emotions that can take decades of secret, at least from him, therapy sessions to try to face, and still not always feel on top of.

Cami reaches out and places a hand on my chest. 'And yet, you're still going to try to send me away.'

My heart sinks as I search her face for anything that says she'll be happy to go. Then it starts to ache, because I know I will do everything in my power to send her away whether she wants it or not. But that's something I decided a long time ago, and I'm not changing it now.

My phone vibrates in my back pocket, and I quickly fish it out.

It's an image of a pale, peach-coloured flower, so full of petals I'm not sure I could count them all.

Sundance: You tell me.

The grin that takes over my face is just about feral, I'm sure of it.

'Well,' Cami drawls, cutting across my thoughts, her hand sliding away. 'Something changed your mood real quick.'

I try to school my features. 'No, nothing,' I stammer. 'Just organising when I'll ride Nightshade again.'

Jamie chuckles from somewhere behind me, and I turn to glare at him. Instead of finding his gaze, though, he's sharing a shit-eating grin with Cami.

Chapter Twenty-Two

TEMPERANCE

Kade: I'm quite confident nothing compares.

With the text, he sends another picture of the gin he gave me that night, and my thighs immediately pull together where I stand in the far paddock. Forcing myself to take a deep breath and focus on the here and now – and not on how Kade's hands felt between my legs – I give Rosie and her growing filly another once-over. I'm happy with how they're both faring and digging into their dinner. The filly is by my other stallion, Loki, and I know in my gut she's going to be a good brood mare, just like her mum.

I'm almost tempted to drive my quad bike over to Loki's paddock and send a photo of him to Kade. But the rest of me is torn between not telling him at all – Loki is a mischief like his namesake, but he's a damn fine horse and will be just as popular as Nightshade once he's trained up – and showing him in person so I can see his reaction.

Instead, I hop back on the quad and head towards the house, my mind wandering back to the night with the gin and how I'm supposed to survive tomorrow's competition so close to Kade without knowing what we're doing. Raising it in a text hasn't felt right, and, so far, every time he's come back to see Nightshade, I haven't been able to see him. Has that been purposeful on his part?

But he's still coming. Still texting. Still working Nightshade. Still, as far as I'm aware, preparing to ride in our next competition. It's an important one – we'll need to get high enough scores to qualify for Nationals – and face Walter Wilder. Again. Kade said he got a free pass on that first ride, and my stomach twists uncomfortably at what Walter will do when he sees Kade ride again, despite being told not to.

My skin prickles in a different way at the statement Kade is making about me and my horse.

Somehow, I've managed to snooze my alarm without being fully conscious of it and am now running really late. Damn it. I scramble out of bed and throw on the clothes I left out last night. Kade will be here in fifteen minutes and I haven't even had coffee. Double damn it. I pull my hair into a braid that will fit under my hat and do the best I can to make myself presentable – something that feels more important than it did last time I saw him ... so I make myself put in less effort. But I still wash my face and put on my favourite day cream, plus a swipe of mascara and blush.

Okay, maybe it was a little more effort than normal.

My phone vibrates in my pocket and I pull it out, finding a text from my dad wishing me luck today. I push away the slightly uncomfortable reminder that I wasn't totally honest with them about Bree, letting them believe she'd be recovered enough from her fall to ride Nightshade. It's not that I think they'd be upset with me about Kade, I just ... I'm not sure how I feel about sharing it with them yet. About the boundaries that would crack.

Kade's truck is already parked outside the round yard. He's brought Nightshade in from the paddock and is getting him settled before loading onto the float. Today's competition is close enough for us to do it in a day – just the next town over, Whimsy Ridge – so he's already in his dress gear. The mostly plain green shirt is dark, like a forest, and it plays against the tan of his hands and neck like it was made for him. Add in his blond beard, dark jeans, broad shoulders, and the hat ...

I just about choke when he turns and smiles at me.

I'm in way over my head and my entire system knows it. I feel like I've swallowed a sparkler.

He gives me a leisurely once-over that warms me from the inside out, like the bloody sparkler has caught fire, and his smile slowly widens.

'Ready for this, Sundance?'

I nod mutely, completely aware I'm lying – I'm not remotely ready for anything with him anymore.

For what should be a disturbing moment, I let myself think about what it would be like to have him here all the time. To introduce him to Loki. To have him train Loki ... I glance towards the other stallion's paddock.

'The sunrise is spectacular from your place,' he murmurs from where he now stands beside me, and I try to quiet the storming in my body at his proximity.

I shouldn't want him to touch me. Be near me. Be imagining him having anything to do with the farm I took over from my grandfather. Just the thought of what his family took from mine – how they went about destroying my grandfather – is enough to make me tremble with rage. Not to mention the fact that I'm risking it all again and Kade doesn't even know.

At the same time, it's undeniable that he's helping me get Nightshade noticed. Without Bree as an option, I needed him ridden, and Kade's skills – not to mention the gossip it's started – means people are paying attention to me and my horse.

My stud.

Kade shifts a little closer, and I soak in the sunrise. He's right – the sun is just starting to light up the sky in pink and orange, promising an incredible day – and it really is spectacular. I used to watch it often as a kid with my family. Underneath, just out of sight from here, the river runs along the border of my place, and I can imagine it reflecting back the colours of the sky.

How it illuminates the now rundown cottage that used to belong to us—

I jump slightly as Kade wraps his free arm around me and pulls me back into him. He feels so warm and strong, and the sense of being held washes over me for a moment. Long enough for me to lean back against his chest despite the nervous hammering of my pulse. There was no hesitation in how he reached for me, gripped me. Clearly my body feels the same, because I'm overcome with a rush of warmth – of … rightness – at being with him in this moment.

'It is beautiful,' I murmur, suddenly aware of how much more mesmerising it is to watch it with someone again.

'I promise, though,' he whispers against my ear, sending shivers down my spine, 'it's not as spectacular as watching you come.'

My cheeks burn as I freeze in place, the warmth of him running the length of mine. Closing my eyes, I hope the relative darkness might somehow undo what he just said. Not because it didn't ignite something in me – but because it did. And I don't know how to shut it off or respond. I'm stuck in a quiet, mortifying moment of thinking I *should* snap back, shut him down. And yet … there's not a single part of me that doesn't want this.

'Well,' I say after too long, 'I hope you enjoyed it. I can't guarantee you'll see it again.'

I step forward and point towards the lightening sky. 'That, however, I *can* assure you you'll see again.'

My words hang in the air between us before I turn and walk around him to the float. Acid burns in my throat with the uncertainty of what I've said and done, and what he's going to take from it when I don't even know myself. My heart is screaming at me not to push him away, but what does that mean for my stud? For what I'm supposed to be doing in my grandad's memory?

What will it mean for Nightshade?

Even being business partners with a Wilder was never on my agenda. Being physically weak to one in *any* way certainly wasn't either. And I'll need every ounce of strength and attention focused on facing Walter Wilder today.

Chapter Twenty-Three

KADE

My fingers itch to touch her again.

But the set of her shoulders tells me I shouldn't, so I grip the steering wheel instead. Force my focus to stay on the road as we head to Whimsy Ridge. I overstepped. I shouldn't have embraced her. I should've known it would be too much.

Fuck, it's a lot for me too.

I've never experienced this sort of clawing under my skin to be close to her – close to *anyone*. To touch her. Hold her. Tell her things.

I roll my lips together. I can do this. So I watched her – *made* her – come, and then I wasn't an asshole the next time I saw her. Sue me. It's not like we can't walk away. We don't have to mention it. No one needs to know, and we can pretend it never happened.

I almost laugh out loud.

There's no way I can pretend the feel of her pussy gripping my fingers won't be featuring in every one of my fantasies for a long damn time. Imagining the other things I could do to hear those sounds from her again.

Shit.

I shift in my seat and drag my mind back to the reining pattern I need to run today. I go through my strategy, and how I want to warm Nightshade up. This competition is crucial – they all are. With only three qualifiers in this part of the state, I need to score well at each one to get us to Nationals. We haven't discussed whether that's our shared goal – it's just been implicit in everything. And we both know she'll need more than the competitions in our region to keep her stud going longer than the short term, and Nightshade's bloodline won't sustain a whole stud on its own anyway.

If I hadn't given away all rights to the Wilder horses, I could've given her a mare or two to use as well. She could get one of them serviced by—

I shut down those thoughts. There's no sense planning like I'll be a permanent fixture in her life. Glancing at her stiff profile, it's clear she wants to get this over with quickly.

The Whimsy Ridge Equestrian Centre is in need of an upgrade. A lot of the facilities in this part of the world do – competitions at this level are not quite what they show in the movies. At the same time, there's a homely, rustic sort of quality about them that makes me feel at home. Despite the plans I have for Wilder Station, and turning it into a state-of-the-art venue, it's actually Riverbow Ranch that gives me the same sense of grounding this place does.

Nightshade stomps down the ramp of the float as she backs him off, murmuring softly to him the whole way.

I wonder if she'd ever murmur to *me* in that same, soft voice?

Stepping aside, I watch as Nightshade completes his short descent, ears flicking at the new sounds, nostrils flaring. He's as calm a stallion as I've ever worked with, but that doesn't mean we should be complacent.

Temperance rubs her palm down his nose as she manoeuvres him around the end of the ramp, while I lift it back into place and latch it.

She waits, Nightshade looking around us, gaze fixed on me as I draw near.

'You know where his stall is?' I ask, knowing she'll have looked at the map and worked out where he needs to be – well away from the mares.

'On the far side, second from the end,' she says, but she doesn't move away.

Instead, she steps towards me, looking up through her dark lashes, and my breath catches. She's close enough for me to pull into my chest again like I did this morning. Except this time, if I did, I'd be within kissing distance.

And kissing Temperance ... fuck. I haven't properly kissed anyone in years. Purposefully. But for a reason that is everything Temperance and not just a kiss, the thought of her mouth on mine is making my dick hard, and she's not even touching me.

Not to mention if word got back to my grandfather, I have no doubt there'd be another punishment – more than just removing me from the horses he knows I love.

She extends Nightshade's lead to me, her hand lifted between us.

'I'll leave you to get connected with him, warm him up. I'll go make sure our registrations are in order and get the run sheet.'

I take the end of the lead, stepping closer again like she's got me hooked on the other end of this rope, and let my fingers brush hers. She holds my gaze as our skin meets, and it burns through something in my chest.

'Okay,' I say. My voice is rough – even I can hear it. Fuck knows what she's making of the effect she has on me.

There's something she's trying to tell me with that long look and our hands held between us, but I can't work out what it is. Is she horrified about the other night? Or worse, ambivalent? Or is she grappling with this feeling in the centre of her chest the same as I am – the one shifting my centre of gravity, and I'm not sure I care?

I pushed the boundaries with her this morning, with both my touch and my words, and she certainly didn't run into the sentiment with open arms.

Should I just ask her? The thought of her shutting down makes a cold sweat break out along my spine.

'You'll be great,' she says, as if each of our careers wasn't riding on these runs of mine. All the same, her confidence in me is comforting – even if it makes my heart beat harder.

As her hand falls away, and I'm still staring stupidly at her, I can't help but wish she wasn't an Archer. Literally anyone else in the world would have been fine.

'Temperance?' Old man Carter says as he approaches, and I wonder how much of our interaction he just caught.

I've had some dealings with him around the edges, but I don't know him well enough to know how kept he is by Walter.

My Sundance smiles at him, a quiet nervousness in her gaze. 'Hi, Ted.'

'I was hoping to talk with you about your stallion.' He flicks me a look that tells me he isn't sure he should be discussing this with her while I'm standing here. But then he nods. 'Kade. Young Cami doing well?'

I mentally shake myself. I have a ride to focus on. And Cami.

Temperance is out of bounds – has put herself out of bounds too – and I need to leave it that way.

'Keeping out of trouble well enough, yeah. I'll leave you to it.' I nod at Temperance, effectively ending our stilted conversation, and forcing a broad smile that conveys far more confidence than I have about keeping things between us platonic.

But this ride I can do. *Have* to do.

So I take Nightshade and walk away from whatever it was Ted interrupted, and I prepare to ride the hell out of her horse – desperately hoping she's about to lock down a service order for Night to sire a foal.

Chapter Twenty-Four

TEMPERANCE

Watching Kade and Nightshade move around the arena like they were made for each other makes my chest tighten. They're both so focused, in tune even after such a short time working together. Kade somehow brings Nightshade to life underneath him, while never losing control of the large, dark beast.

Sand flies from beneath Nightshade's hooves as they drive from one end of the arena to the other, coming to a sliding stop that lasts several breaths.

Beside me, Marlowe lets out a loud 'whoop', and I drop my head to cover my grin. That man, on my horse, does things to me that should be a sin. At the very least, it certainly makes me think about sinful things.

'Have you thought more about that?' she asks quietly, tipping her head towards the arena while looking at me. 'If he' – she points at Kade – 'was literally *anybody* else's option, they wouldn't hesitate. You know that, right?'

I laugh half-heartedly as I push back from the barrier separating owners and riders at the arena. Marlowe mirrors the movement and falls in beside me. Her glossy black braid is similar to mine beneath her hat, but hers isn't coated in dirt like mine always is. Sometimes I envy that she has another life outside the land – but then again, I can't imagine living any other way.

'I'm serious,' she presses, her tone losing its earlier lightness. 'Maybe you need to give it a go. What would be so bad if you and Kade—'

I glance around, pulse spiking, and shush her. 'There isn't anything,' I say quietly. 'And what would be *so bad*? His grandfather threatened to ruin me if I seduced his grandson. You know as well as I do that man has the means to follow through. I just got my first official interest' – excitement wars with dread – 'and I can't risk that now. If Walter ...'

She releases a frustrated sigh. 'Asshole,' she mutters, crossing her arms as she narrows her eyes at Kade, who approaches on Nightshade. The attendants open the gate, close it behind him, and the air in my lungs compresses as he smiles – focused solely on me – as he rides forward.

I smile up at him, my hat tipping back. 'That was so good,' I breathe. 'Truly, Kade – really good.'

He nudges Nightshade a step closer so I'm level with his shoulder and Kade's leg, his muscled thigh gripping my horse. Leaning down, he catches the brim of my hat, holding my head gently in place as I gaze up at him.

'Sundance,' he murmurs, not quite close enough for his breath to touch my skin, but close enough for me to see every gold fleck in his navy eyes, 'that was better than fucking "good", and we both know it.'

He releases my hat and runs the pad of his thumb along the hollow of my cheekbone, from my ear to the corner of my mouth, and goosebumps break out in places I never imagined possible.

I stand frozen as Kade rides off with Nightshade, blinking into the suddenly vacant space before me. He's right – it *was* better than good. But it's not his ride that has desire prickling across my entire body. It's his ... everything. The look in his eyes when he takes me in, the brush of his breath on my skin, how wholeheartedly he's thrown himself into this with me, the feel of his hands on my body ... between my legs.

It's the undeniable knowledge that he's not just referring to his ride.

I suppress a shiver as Marlowe clears her throat.

Fuuuck.

'Peri, babe.' She grips my shoulders and turns me to face her, dark brows drawn low. 'I just about combusted on the spot being in the same vicinity as the two of you.' She glances over her shoulder towards where Kade disappeared. 'I get that it's going to be super complicated but, Wilder or not, that look does *not* come around every day. Whatever his grandfather could – *would* – do, you know I've got your back, right?'

My shoulders drop a little, and her hands move with me.

'What if it's not him who does the destroying?' I whisper.

Because that thought won't leave me alone.

My attraction to Kade is undeniable. But that one slip-up in my kitchen – I could forget that. Explain it away with gin. Anything more, though, and I'll look like an absolute fool.

But what troubles me most isn't that he's the most gorgeous man I've ever laid eyes on, or that my senses respond to him like they've been waiting for him.

It's the way images of him in my life have started creeping in. How being with him feels natural. Welcome. How I even enjoyed spending time with Jamie and Cami.

What troubles me is how powerless I might be to stop the inevitable train wreck. How much I might be like my grandad – and give him everything, only for Kade to leave me destitute.

Chapter Twenty-Five

TEMPERANCE

Unsurprisingly, Kade does well in the next two events – finishing overall second for the day, and qualifying us for the last regional event we need. The scores aren't important except for what they do for the rankings. It's consistency I want. For Nightshade to be seen taking these events in his stride, regardless of their diversity. Whether he's completing a reining pattern or working cow, I want the audience – and the wealthier breeders, dealers, and trainers – to see how damn special he is, and start imagining what his bloodline could do for their futures.

Just like Ted Carter.

But that doesn't mean the thrill of Kade's second place isn't rubbing off on me as well. He's elated, and the joy is contagious – doubly so with Ted wanting to see my fees and terms to breed from Nightshade. He'd be an invaluable supporter if I can land him.

'You're *gloating*,' I mock-admonish once we're finally back in the truck and on our way home.

He laughs out loud, a genuine, unguarded sound that pulls one from me too. 'Yeah,' he says, 'I guess I am. I've spent so long being told I could never do this – never be out in front and do it well ...' His voice trails off, a slight edge creeping into his happiness.

'You believed it,' I finish.

He gives me an indecipherable look before returning his attention to the road. 'I think ... sometimes you can be told something enough that it becomes a truth in itself, yes,' he replies, and I can't shake the feeling he's talking about something else as well.

My chest pounds with the need to face this head-on now. We've started working together. He's literally had his hands in my pants and makes my heart race. I've shared his bed.

And yet we've said nothing about any of that. Or about the threat his grandfather poses. Does he care about that anymore? Or are his ties so irrevocably cut that it's no longer a concern? Would he care that his family can still undo me?

'Like what?' I ask gently, referring to his statement, trying to dig in a little.

'Like ... how much people's surnames define them.'

My breath leaves me in a rush, despite this being exactly where I wanted the conversation to go. 'Meaning?'

For a few long moments, the only sounds are his truck rolling along the highway and the soft hum of country music filling the dim cab.

'Meaning I don't think I've met your expectations of me.'

I draw back, the accuracy of his words hitting me square in the chest. Watching the road instead of his shadowed outline, I run the statement through my mind, its implications making my skin heat.

'What about your expectations of me?'

He gives a low chuckle. 'That's a bit of a "yes" and "no" one. I've always known you weren't what my grandfather tried to make you out to be.' He gives me a pointed sideways glance. 'We might not have been friends in school, Temperance, but I'm not completely fucking ignorant.'

I try to breathe around the knot in my throat. 'And the other bit?' I press, unable to directly ask what, exactly, has been outside his expectations.

He runs a hand up the back of his neck, a move I have a sudden desire to follow – to feel his skin there, to reassure him I can take whatever he's about to say.

But is that true?

Blowing out a forceful breath, he pulls his shoulders back.

'The other bit started the night Juniper came to my bar. The night I found you in the storeroom. That night, you blew all of my expectations out the fucking window.'

I go still.

I don't know what I expected him to say, but acknowledging that night in the storeroom did something to him that's *still* in play – something perhaps beyond the fact that I'm still holding that rope, like he told me before – feels ... like a lot. A good *lot* that makes my stomach giddy and my thighs itch to press together to soothe some of the gentle pressure building there. A *lot* that's also pegged in by layers of *what the fuck* and *how do I do this* and *what if Walter Wilder* ...

But I want Kade. That's been clear for some time, even if I still find it hard to reconcile.

And it seems he's on the same trajectory as me.

Too soon, my driveway comes into view and Kade slows steadily, the weight of the gooseneck towing Nightshade pressing in slightly. He takes the corner with the level of care I've come to expect, and we drive the rest of the way to the barn in silence. The thumping in my chest is loud in my ears.

Coming to a stop in the dark, I watch the dust swirl in the headlights.

Neither of us gets out.

Kade shifts slightly in his seat as he turns to look at me, the full attention of his gaze burning into my side. When I meet his look, my heart somersaults in my chest. He's mostly in shadow, partly illuminated by the headlights through the windscreen and the sensor light on the barn. Just enough for me to see the outline of his beard and shoulders. The side of his nose. One half of his full mouth—

I lift my gaze back to his eyes, which look almost midnight blue in this light.

'You're right,' I say softly, breaking the silence. 'You're not entirely what I expected, no.'

But how do I tell him his grandfather is still the asshole I've always known him to be? That his hatred for my family is so strong he's prepared to ruin me the same way he ruined my grandfather?

He doesn't move.

'But,' I whisper, 'your grandfather was very clear with me – now that you've ridden again, he'll try to ruin Riverbow Stud. If he thinks I ...'

Kade goes rigid in his seat, any hint of ease gone from his body.

'If you what?' he asks tightly.

'If ... he thinks I've attempted to seduce you in any way, he'll take everything from me. I wouldn't even have the ranch, or a place for my flowers, or—'

A loud, harsh laugh rips from his throat, but it sounds agonised enough to strike a painful blow to my chest. He tips his head towards the window before twisting back in his seat, away from me, gripping the steering wheel.

'Temperance,' he murmurs after a long beat, 'I—' He shakes his head. 'I don't actually know what to say.' He sighs heavily. 'We should unload Night.'

I watch him get out of the truck, the heavy shut of his door sealing me in. I'm not sure what I expected his reaction to be, but his seemingly resigned acceptance – that this might be the end of whatever was happening here – is ... disconcerting.

What if I *want* to seduce Kade?

For genuine, thrilling, terrifying reasons.

What if I want to be seduced by him?

Then what?

Sliding from the truck, I round the back of the gooseneck just as Nightshade steps off the ramp. I watch Kade walk 'Night', as he keeps calling him, towards the paddock gate beyond the round yard. He murmurs something I can't hear, strokes his nose, then removes the halter and lets him wander off.

Kade stands there a long time, his back to me, right on the line where the barn light ends. When he finally turns, I duck into the tack room to unpack.

We work in silence. Replacing Nightshade's saddle, saddle blanket, halters and bridles, and more brushes and gear than I remember packing. Nightshade clearly has more personal items than I do.

And with every trip I make, my palms start to sweat a little more. Not because I'm already covered in dirt and sand and horse after a long day, but because every trip takes me closer to Kade leaving. I can't tell if he'd be leaving with unfinished business between us, or if getting out of the truck when he did *was* the end of it.

Kade's biceps flex under his shirt as he places Night-shade's secondary, backup saddle on its rack. He's so close I can almost feel him beside me, the warmth of him seeping into the space between us. Surrounded by worn, warm timber walls, and every variety of leather horse equipment I can imagine, I realise there's some-thing so natural about him being in this space – some-thing that acts like a hook beneath my sternum, linking me to him.

My pulse hammers in my ears.

What would he do if I just reached out and touched him?

He straightens, hands still braced on the saddle, and I study his profile before he glances sideways at me.

We wash our hands at the simple sink I had installed when I first took over, the tension in the air thickening across my skin.

'I think that's everything,' he says quietly, the timbre of his voice washing over me, just like it did that day in the storeroom.

His beard moves with his words, and I can't help but reach out and softly take the end of it, turning his head towards me. His brows quirk in question, but he doesn't stop me. He just studies me as he leans into me. Less than a hand's breadth separates us.

'He didn't say anything would happen if *you* seduced *me*,' I whisper, painfully aware of how humiliated I'll be if he doesn't return the sentiment. But that doubtful voice in my head is so quiet compared to the rising beat in my chest telling me to trust it. *Feel* it.

Kade's eyes darken, but he still doesn't say anything as I release his beard, letting my hands fall to his chest. Heat floods my cheeks, and I tear my gaze away, staring instead at the stretch of chest between his shoulders.

He takes a tiny step forward – close enough to easily grip my hips, close enough that we're almost chest to chest. If my breaths were any deeper, my breasts would brush him. Still, I focus on the small white buttons with green fabric that run down the centre of his now dusty riding shirt.

'Would you want that?' he asks, his breath tickling the wild strands of hair escaping the top of my braid.

Any words I could say scatter like startled birds, fleeing my mind to race laps around the round yard. I look up into his face, into the burning intensity in his gaze that makes me feel like I'm the only person in the world.

He steps in again, this time pressing his hips to mine, and backing me against the wall. The halters hanging from the hooks above my head drape down on either side of me, brushing my shoulders.

'Temperance,' he murmurs, and I have to suppress a groan at how my body responds to the way he says my name. 'I asked you a question.'

I swallow. 'What was it again?' I tease, though my chest is rising too hard and fast for me to even pretend at a smile.

Kade slides a hand along my jaw, tipping my head to the side as he leans towards my ear.

'I asked if you would want me to seduce you.'

His words are velvet and sandpaper on my skin, my nipples tightening in my bra. Weakness floods my knees as need pulses through me, and I all but whimper.

'Please, Kade.'

Chapter Twenty-Six

KADE

I still. Giddy on the scent of her hair – like strawberries just picked, sweet and a little dirty. It takes a moment for her words to sink in, to travel from my throbbing groin to my brain.

Beneath my hand, Temperance shifts slightly, further exposing her neck. I take the invitation and lick up the column of her throat. She inhales quickly, as if I've surprised her, and then lets out a quiet whimper as I swirl my tongue before kissing her just behind her ear.

'Sundance,' I whisper against her silken skin. The subtle tremor that goes through her when I say her name never gets old. 'Given how wet I'm quite confident you are right now, I'd say the seducing has already begun.'

She huffs a laugh, eyes closed. 'Let's see if the seduction's been worth it, then.' She peeks up at me, and the look she gives goes straight to my dick so fast I feel precum leaking into my jocks.

Fuck, she's gorgeous. And warm. And smart. And ...

I'm headed in a really fucking dangerous direction with her. But with her pressed between me and the wall, literally open for my taking, there's nothing I can do but hope I survive the fallout.

Her hands roam my chest as I take her earlobe between my teeth and nip before returning to her neck, trailing open-mouthed kisses down along her collarbones. She pushes her chest into me, hands on my ribs and grinding her pussy against me, and I slowly undo her top three buttons.

Just enough for the creamy skin of her breasts to spill forward, framed by her checked shirt and straining against her black bra. Taking one in each hand, I trace my thumbs over the tops of them – her skin so much softer than mine – and watch the deepening rise and fall of her chest. I can feel her gaze and lift mine to meet it.

There's a seriousness in her features that hits me right in the gut. A vulnerability that pulls sharply in my chest. A sense of belonging that floods my veins in a way nothing else ever has. I place a kiss to the top of each breast as Temperance moans and tangles her fingers in my hair, then inhale deeply in the valley between them.

Temperance presses her hips into me harder, and I have to bite the inside of my lip at the pressure building in my cock. Stepping back slightly, I lock eyes with her again as I undo, then remove, my belt.

'Do you trust me?' I rasp, pulse racing.

Her eyes flick to the thick leather belt hanging from my hand before rising back to my face.

She nods.

Without looking away, I loop my belt through itself into a figure eight and hold it out towards her with both hands.

'Give me your hands.'

Heat flares in her gaze as she takes in the pseudo handcuffs, then slowly drags her eyes up my chest, over my mouth, and finally meets my stare again.

She holds out her hands.

Biting my teeth together and desperately trying to talk my dick into not blowing right now, I slip the leather over her wrists and tighten the strap. I remove the bridle from the hook closest to her head and gently lift her arms so I can loop my belt over the hook instead.

She's not completely restrained – we both know it. But we stand there, panting, staring at each other. The image of her: arms overhead, anchored to the wall, my belt around her wrists, standing on her tiptoes with her shirt undone and breasts exposed *for me* – that's going to stay with me until I die.

I run a hand over my face, feeling the coarse hair of my beard. 'You're the most gorgeous thing I've ever laid eyes on, Sundance.'

'Kade,' she whispers, desperation clinging to her, and I can't help but grin.

I make a low, noncommittal sound in my throat, tipping my head as I watch her heavy-lidded eyes flutter when I run a finger under the fabric of her bra and rub her nipple.

She groans, the sound itself a shot of pleasure, and I palm her right breast, bending to take her hard nipple into my mouth through her bra. My Sundance writhes on the spot as I grip that same nipple lightly between my teeth.

'Fuck, Kade,' she breathes, tugging a little at the restraint of my belt and thrusting her hips towards me, finding my thigh.

'Yes, Sundance?' I ask slowly, giving her other breast the same treatment.

Her head tips back against the wall, and I listen to the vibration of her moan. Releasing her nipple, I move to her jeans, unbuttoning and sliding them down her legs. I catch the heel of her boots on the way, pulling them off inside the denim, letting the tangle fall to the floor. Temperance's thighs are tense as I drag my hands over her pale skin – skin scattered with freckles almost as soft as she is.

I grip her legs, one hand on each side, transfixed as my tan fingers sink into her hot flesh. Dropping to my knees, I run my nose up the dark, damp fabric of her panties and take a deep inhale. She smells different here – more decadent somehow – and I rub myself through my jeans.

Balanced on her toes, her movement is limited, and she whimpers when I pull my face away, tilting her hips towards me. I hook my fingers under the edge of her panties where they meet her right thigh and drag the back of my knuckles over her.

Her mouth falls open in an 'O' as I apply a little more pressure.

'I need you,' she gasps, voice strangled. 'Please, Ka—'

I press the pads of two fingers against her entrance. 'Here?'

'Oh, fuck – yes. There. Please.'

Slowly, I remove my hand and rise to stand before her.

'Look at me,' I instruct.

She blinks her eyes open, her whole being fogged with desire.

But she doesn't meet my eyes. Instead, she watches my hands as I undo the button on my jeans and free my rock-fucking-hard cock.

I fist myself, and her breath catches.

Squeezing my dick, I will myself – again – not to come too soon. Closing the small gap between us, I rip her underwear in half and run the head of my cock through her folds. The soft heat of her almost takes me back to my knees.

Breathing hard through my nose, I take my wallet from my back pocket, find the condom I keep there for opportunities that have never felt anything like this, and sheath myself.

With one last look to confirm she still wants this, I bury myself in Temperance Archer.

She calls out, her back arching as her hips press hard against me, demanding I take her deeper, her toes scrambling on the dusty floor. I grip the back of her thighs and lift her until her legs wrap around me and I have her pinned against the wall once more.

A handful of words fall from her mouth, but all I can make out is *more* as I drive myself – over and over – into her. Her tight, wet, slick pussy feels like a home I never could have imagined.

She starts to tremble in my grip, her thighs squeezing as they shake, the back of her shirt riding up as she slides against the wall. I widen my stance so she can use my hips for purchase and slip a hand between us, pinching her clit.

'Kade,' she chokes out, 'harder – I – hard—'

If it weren't for the surge of ecstasy powering up my spine and through my limbs, I'd almost think the world had stopped as Temperance comes around me. Her cries fall in time with the soft jerking of her body as her pleasure shudders through her, the walls of her pussy pulsing again and again.

I circle her clit firmly as I move within her, dragging out her orgasm even as mine has already taken my breath.

When I feel strong enough to move my arms, I release hers from my belt, running my fingers gently over her wrists and kissing them as I listen to the leather slip off the hook, the buckle hitting the floor. Snaking my arms around her back, she drops her head to my chest. I keep her pinned between me and the wall, her legs still around my waist, my slowly softening cock still inside her.

Resting my chin on the top of her head, I hold her like I will never let her go.

Chapter Twenty-Seven

TEMPERANCE

Slowly, I ease my legs from Kade's hips and slide myself down his front, standing before him in just my thick work socks and a half-open shirt. And a ruined pair of underwear. Apart from the fact that I know his jeans are undone, Kade is completely dressed.

I place my palms on his chest and look up into his face. 'We should get cleaned up,' I say quietly.

He cups my face in his hands, threading his fingers into my hair again. A wave of goosebumps tumble down my neck at the sensation. I close my eyes and smile – one I'm sure gives away just how much bliss is still pouring through me.

'I like this face,' he whispers, his breath fanning my cheeks.

'Because I'm the "most gorgeous thing" you've ever laid eyes on?' I murmur, acutely aware of the rich, post-orgasm timbre of my voice.

Kade laughs softly, and a luxurious warmth begins its way back down my limbs, reigniting what had started to settle into immense comfort.

'Because it's pure, unguarded you ... and I put it there.'

My chest squeezes as I blink up at him.

'Ask me to stay, Temperance,' he whispers. Quietly. Like he's afraid I might say no.

I study him, a sliver of mental clarity sharpening the fog in my mind, and become aware of my lips – slightly swollen, begging to be kissed. My heart thumps between my ribs. I stretch up into his chest and place a kiss on the side of his mouth, his beard tickling my skin.

'Kade,' I breathe, moving to whisper into his ear. 'I want you to stay with me tonight.'

I watch him swallow.

'Let's get you in the shower,' he says.

The walk from my barn to the house is dark and a little chilly. One we do in silence, but it's brimming with something that fills my chest with butterflies. There's a voice in the back of my mind asking what the hell I just did with Kade Wilder, but it's nowhere near as loud as my previous objections to him. Instead, there's a growing awareness of just how wrong that voice is turning out to be.

Nowhere in Kade have I seen even a semblance of his grandfather. Never has he given me cause to doubt his intentions here are anything but mutual. He's never overstepped or pried or snooped around my farm as if he could destroy whatever progress I'm making.

No.

I glance sideways at him, the crinkles at the corners of his eyes just beginning to appear as the sensor light outside my kitchen door clicks on. Wordlessly, he takes my hand as we make the last steps to the side door of the farmhouse. His thumb strokes the back of my hand as he comes to a stop, gently pulling me into him.

'Temperance,' he murmurs, lifting his other hand to my face. I lean into his palm and let the spark of the connection settle through me. 'You know if we do this, we can't go back.'

I search his face, unsure what exactly he means, and jerk my head a little in the direction of the barn.

'You mean that was ...' I frown. We've already *done it*.

'I mean,' he says, blowing out a short, tense breath, 'that could have been a fit of passion.'

My brows rise, but he's not wrong.

'But *this*,' he continues, 'me walking through that door with the intention of staying ... that has the potential to bring us both down.'

'More than denying you your legacy with those horses?'

His features fracture a little. 'I'm less worried about that than I am about Cami's. Or yours.'

I nod. 'He's a powerful man.'

Neither of us needs to say who. I reach up, take the hand he has on my face, link our fingers, and bring our joined hands between us.

'I understand if you don't want this enough,' I say quietly. 'I really do. And I promise not to add it to my "reasons I hate Kade Wilder" list.' I smile and hope it doesn't seem as thin as it feels.

He lifts a brow. 'There's a list?'

I smile. 'It's pretty long.'

He laughs, though something darker threads through the sound. 'Sundance, I'm trying to tell you we have a choice to make – have tonight, and whatever comes after, and face the consequences of Walter Wilder. Or walk away and keep a truce for us and future generations. But … you're saying the choice is to see this through or leave you with your "reasons to hate me" list?'

Ignoring the compression in my ribs is hard as I hold his gaze. As I try not to let him see how vulnerable I am to all of this – and how little choice I actually have when it comes to how I feel about him.

'I'm saying' – my words careful and slow – 'that I don't think we should let anyone, including old men, bully us. But I also understand that's a much easier thing for *me* to say when I'm not that man's family.'

He releases my hands and slides his around my back, drawing us flush together. The breeze tickles my hair and bare legs as my palms roam his torso, like they have a mind of their own and can't get enough of him.

'So you don't care if I'm a disgraced Wilder?'

Now it's my turn to laugh. 'I think I might even prefer that.'

He smiles, and I trace his lips with my fingertips, the desire to kiss him building in more places than I can count.

'Something tells me that if I was ever able to turn you down, it'd be the death of me,' he murmurs against my fingers.

I rise onto my toes, pressing into him, relishing the feel of my breasts against his chest even through our clothes. 'Time to go inside,' I whisper, placing a kiss just below his ear. Then I reach around, open the door, and stumble us both into the kitchen.

My bathroom is full of steam as Kade runs my shower and I undress. His gaze darkens as I become increasingly exposed, and a heady sense of power flows through my veins. He sits on the edge of the tub while I step into the shower, sighing deeply as the hot water hits my skin. I love what I do outside all day, but I also adore being clean. More than that, being watched by the most impossibly attractive man silently cataloguing every feature of me has me so turned on I think I might explode.

I let my hands trail down my body, gently washing every inch of skin, but my touch only makes my blood run hotter. When I glance at Kade as I run my washcloth over my breasts, I find him white-knuckling the edge of the bath with a very obvious hard-on straining against his jeans. I smile into the water and drag the cloth over my stomach, drifting my hands down between my legs.

'Do it,' he commands, voice rough.

My breath catches, but I do as I'm told and run my fingers up and down my slit. I'm warm, slightly swollen, and my breasts feel heavier. A sound breaks in the back of my throat as I slide my fingers inside myself, drawing back out to circle my clit. But right now, I know this will never be enough.

So I turn fully to Kade, still cupping myself, and find his gaze through the increasingly wet shower screen. 'I don't want to do this alone.'

'Fuck,' he mutters, rising from the edge of the tub and stripping. His movements are slow and measured, but the look on his face suggests he's fighting to be so – and I can't help the grin that curves my lips.

I'm struck speechless when he steps through the shower door and crowds me in. He's all golden-brown skin and muscles, quickly slick with water, and a dark, hungry gaze that drinks me in. His dick is hard and proud, and my pussy throbs at the sight of it – knowing exactly how well he can use it.

Emboldened by his earlier commands, I tell him to palm himself while I watch, every sense narrowing to the movement of his hand stroking up and down his cock. The muscles of his forearm flex, sending heat racing through me. I whimper, need pulsing thick and heavy, and reach out to catch his wrist.

'Stop,' I say, the shower still beating down on me. 'I want it.'

He steps deeper into the shower, pressing into me and shoving me back against the cold tiled wall. I gasp as he leans into the crook of my neck.

'Greedy little thing, aren't you?' he teases, smiling into my skin before nipping at it.

I groan, head falling back on the tiles as he grinds against me. 'Fuck, Kade. Please. I just – want—'

'Temperance,' he whispers, my skin pebbling despite the heat of the water, 'I will never be able to deny you anything when you say *please*.'

My breath stutters at his admission, my mind suddenly full of all the things I could decide to ask for. But right now, I just want to be filled by Kade. Want to feel him move within me. Want to feel him come apart as hard as I do. I want to know his world is as tipped off its axis as mine.

'Please,' I repeat.

'Turn around and show me your ass.'

I spin, plant my hands on the wall, and push my hips back towards him. It lasts only a moment before he grips my hips and nudges at my entrance. Heat floods me, and I can't keep my eyes open. Tilting my hips higher, Kade drives into me and I cry out, the sensation overwhelming.

Every slam of his cock – deeper than I thought possible – winds me tighter and tighter, and all I can do is whimper as the desperate need to break edges closer.

Kade fists my wet hair as he pumps faster, his other hand digging into the flesh of my hip. He lets out a strangled sound as he tugs me back by the hair – firm but controlled – so my back arches into his chest. Still, he thrusts up into me, forcing me onto my tiptoes. His free hand slides down to my clit and circles with just the right pressure, sending shockwaves through me as I cry out, the intensity building so high I almost can't take it.

Then it shatters – violent, blissful – wracking through me and leaving me breathless. Without releasing his hold on me, Kade pulls out and presses his cock between us. He moans, deep and wrecked, as hot jets of cum spill across my back, amongst the shower water, and drip down my ass.

Chapter Twenty-Eight

KADE

I drop my head to Temperance's shoulder for long moments before I have to stand properly and tuck her into me instead, lowering my chin to the top of her head. Her chest heaves under my forearms, and I squeeze her tighter. There's a desperate, almost primal part of me that wants to turn her slowly, look into her breathtaking face, and kiss her.

Having her mouth on mine, tasting her lips ... it feels like the final piece.

Which is exactly why I don't do it. Not yet.

I have no idea where this is going – until that night in the storeroom, I would *never* have thought we'd end up here. Since then, though, both of our lives have been tipped upside down, in large part because of the other, and I don't want to scare her. Or push her too hard. Discovering Temperance like this – wet and hot against me, yes – but also soft and open and supportive and looking at me like I matter is ... enough to make my chest feel like Nightshade has stepped on it.

I can't give her the final piece of me as well – what if I never come back from that? What if she thinks that's too much right now?

So I focus on washing her completely off, spreading the water over her back and down her ass with my hands, removing all evidence that I just came all over her in her shower. Erasing it brings a certain kind of loss to me too. One that makes me want to immediately mark her up somehow so the whole world knows she belongs to—

I clamp down on that thought and kiss up the back of her neck instead, savouring the way she moans and sinks further into me, letting me support her in the downpour.

'Are you hungry?' she asks, her voice still laced with satisfaction.

Satisfaction that makes my dick start to harden again. But there's a sleepy undertone too, and god knows we could both use some rest after hauling around at the show all day.

I reach around her and turn off the taps, guiding her out of the shower and grabbing the dark sort-of-pink towel from the rack. She watches me as I dry her off, her eyelids drooping but her focus never wavering.

'If you keep looking at me like that,' I say as I work my way down her legs, cock now well and truly hard again, 'we're never going to get out of this bathroom.'

She smiles, the gesture so full of warmth the inside of my chest grows several sizes. 'I could get on board with that,' she teases.

Her lips are pink and soft – I know from when she's kissed my body – and I have to force myself to look away. If she notices, she doesn't say.

'But you're right. I think my bed is calling. You get dry,' she says, pressing the now-damp towel into my hands, 'and I'll make us a snack.'

'You know what didn't help my assessment of you – the part that was all you?'

I quirk a brow at her as she moves the now-empty cheese platter to her bedside table.

'It wasn't enough that our grandfathers hated each other?' I ask.

'I was too young to really understand what was coming, back then,' she replies. 'And that's not a guess.'

'Right,' I drawl. 'So, just to be clear, while we're both naked in your bed, you want me to work out what I did to make you hate me?'

'Yup.' She smiles slyly, as she slides down the bed and places her head on the pillow.

I prop myself on an elbow and reach out, letting my fingers drift through her hair while I think over every interaction we've ever had. She said she was 'young'.

'So you're thinking of something in school?' I ask.

She nods, and I frown. We were never friends in school, and we kept a respectable distance from each other. Some of our friends overlapped – like Jamie and Marlowe –

but Marlowe didn't come until later, and keeping track of who's connected to who isn't helping me crack this.

Every now and then someone would catch on to the feud between our families – knowledge likely passed down from their parents or grandparents – and try to stir shit up, but mostly we ignored it. Enough that I have absolutely no clue what she's referring to.

And the not knowing has already started to eat at me. I know she can't seriously still be hung up on whatever it was – not after we started working together with Night – but the idea that even a tiny part of her might still hate me is more of a sharp shard than I'd like to admit.

'Okay,' I concede, 'I don't know. What was it?'

She studies me, and for a second I think she won't actually tell me. I give her hair a gentle tug.

'Sundance, you're killing me. You can't still hate me.'

She pulls a face that makes me want to fuck her immediately, and also constricts my breath – because maybe she really does still hate me.

'You didn't invite me to your birthday parties,' she says, voice soft and full of confession.

I blink at her.

'Every other girl would go, swooning over Kade fucking Wilder, and I never even got an invite.'

I stare, a distressed kind of laughter bursting out of me. 'Holy shit,' I gasp as she shoves me in the chest. 'You can't be serious?'

She narrows her gaze, cheeks flushing. 'No need to rub it in, asshole.'

Shaking my head, I try to make sense of it. 'Were you *jealous*?'

'Of you? Not at all,' she answers – and I believe her completely. 'But you made me a complete pariah – swung everyone to the Wilder side without even trying. There were very few people prepared to see my side of the story after that.'

I let that sink in. Part of me can see what she's saying, but the truth is, I hated those parties. They were never for me – they were opportunities for my grandfather to flaunt himself. So ... I guess what she's saying is right. Whether he knew how personally she'd take it or not, I was a vehicle for him to manipulate everyone around us.

There's a smudge of hurt in her eyes, and I don't blame her. As much as I want this not to be an issue between us – as much as I want to take whatever this is as far as it will go, something I've *never* wanted with anyone before – I can still see it there.

Neither of us can outrun the fact that my grandfather treated their common horses appallingly, cheated by drugging them, and pinned it on hers – effectively screwing him out of a stud. Or that he's lied about it for so long I think he even believes it now. Or that he then had land boundaries moved by the council he sits on to take a piece of property the Archers could have made revenue from.

And we certainly can't ignore the fact that he's still threatening her.

She might not have told me everything about when he cornered her in the stables, but it was written all over her face – whatever he said made her very uncomfortable. And uncomfortable is one thing, but I know how quickly he can press that into pain of another kind. My heart rate kicks up several notches thinking of the ways he could hurt her because of me, and I clench my teeth together for a moment. Remind myself where I am. That I can keep her safe.

I scoot a little closer, leaning down over her until our noses are almost touching, but I can still see her eyes. Stunning, deep green eyes framed by mid-brown lashes.

'For what it's worth, I wanted to invite you to my parties. I paid ... a lot' – I try to smother my wince at the memory of the sting in the back of my legs when he said no – 'because I asked to have you there.' I can see the questions rising in her features, so I plough on; I need to get this out anyway. 'My relationship with him has been ... tumultuous,' I say, knowing it's a completely inadequate way to describe it. As I think on it – and Sundance watches me, patiently waiting – I realise I've only ever talked about this out loud with my therapist. I don't think I have the words to tell Temperance what it was like.

She places her hand over my heart, and I breathe into the warmth blooming beneath her palm. 'You don't have to tell me,' she whispers, and I shake my head.

'He was ... very abusive, but I'm – I'm not like that, Temperance. I need you to—'

My Sundance shifts her hand and places a finger on my lips. 'I know.'

I study her auburn hair on her checked pillowcase as I compose myself, her words – *I know* – landing like hot lava in my chest.

'I offered myself gladly much of the time,' I say against her fingertips, 'because while-ever I was his outlet for rage, it wasn't Cami. And I just ... I really needed it not to be Cami.'

Temperance moves her hand again, this time cupping the back of my head, threading her fingers through my hair as she softly presses her mouth to my forehead.

'I'm not going to make you relive it, Kade,' she says quietly. 'But I'm here anytime you want to talk, okay?'

Silently, I nod, and we hold each other as the world seems to shift itself around us. Shift and rearrange.

Eventually, I clear my throat. 'To be abundantly clear, though, I *am* inviting you to this party.'

She laughs, even if something tentative hides beneath it. Wriggling her hands out from the covers, she runs them over my chest and down my ribs, scratching lightly with her nails and forcing my eyes to flutter closed at the sensation.

'Well,' she murmurs, arching her neck and offering it to my mouth, 'if this is our party, let's enjoy it.'

Chapter Twenty-Nine

TEMPERANCE

I can barely contain my smile as I join my regular video chat with Marlowe and Juniper. There's no way they won't notice the shift in my mood, and I'm not sure I care. Being with Kade is freeing in a way I would never have expected – not from him. Not from anyone, really. Trusting people when you're an Archer can be hard, and this … thing with Kade has blown everything out of the water. His warmth, his vulnerability with me, his … everything has me in a complete spin.

Adjusting the cushions on my couch, I stretch out and prop my phone on the edge so I can lie on my side and wait for them to join.

Juniper's megawatt smile pops up first, followed by the jerky blur of sky and tall buildings behind her. She's clearly walking somewhere, earphones in, multitasking.

'Hi, beautiful,' she greets, glancing down at her phone while navigating the footpath. 'Do we have Marlowe yet?'

'Not—'

'Sorry I'm late,' Marlowe says by way of greeting.

'Babe' – Juniper rolls her eyes – 'we've literally been here for ten seconds, that's not late.'

'Well,' Marlowe mutters, brushing her dark hair from her face, 'you'd know.'

Juniper laughs. 'Okay, I don't have long today, sorry – tell me everything. When do you see Henry again, Lowie?'

Marlowe is quiet for a beat too long, and I narrow my eyes at her on the screen. She sighs. 'Next month, probably. But ... I'm not sure I'm sad about that. We don't need to live in each other's pockets.'

I watch Juniper tilt her head as she tries to keep the phone steady. 'What does "not sad" mean, babe?'

'I don't know, I just ... I feel a little less anxious when I'm here on my own.'

'Marlowe,' I say gently, 'that's a pretty big deal. You shouldn't feel anxious about your partner.'

She closes her eyes a fraction. 'I know, and I'm not down, I promise – I think it's just a symptom of long-distance, you know? There's so much pressure to have everything perfect when we're together. It's just ... less stressful when we're not. But I love him, and we're good. Forget I said anything.'

I meet Juniper's gaze on the chat, and I know neither of us will let that go for long. But if there's anything we know about Marlowe, it's that she needs to work things through on her own first – at least initially – and then we weigh in.

'Linden said you're loving being back in the Valley,' Juniper cuts in.

'I am. I might even buy here. You two were holding out on me – this is the sweetest little town ever, even as an adult. I should've come back much sooner.'

Juniper and I laugh. 'Yeah, if you can escape the small-town drama,' I add. 'School was one thing, Marlowe – being a permanent adult resident is quite another.'

'Oh!' Juniper squeals. 'You HAVE to move there forever!'

My heart swells. 'Junie, please come home – we could all be here,' I say with a smile, knowing how massively her music career is taking off and how unlikely it is she'll be a Blackwood Valley resident any time soon.

She sighs wistfully. 'If only. At least then I'd be able to kiss the squishy cheeks of that little Coco. Are you two keeping a good eye on Linden?'

'Yeah,' I reply. 'Honestly, he makes me so proud, but it's tough. All of it's tough – his own grief, supporting his mum, raising Coco. Even with us, and the great team he and his mum make, I think it's pretty isolating.'

We're all quiet for a moment, but this isn't new. The loss of Linden's sister hit us all hard. Now it's about the three of us supporting him as best we can. But often it feels like there's only so much Marlowe and I can do – Juniper is his best friend and, while I know he'd never stop her living her dreams, it's always clear how much he misses her. For the same reasons, Marlowe and I don't tell her that, either.

'He's coming tonight, though,' Marlowe adds. 'His mum will take Coco, and we're going to have dinner at Jamie's. You're coming too, right, Peri?'

My mouth gapes a little. Dinner at Jamie's? Where Kade currently lives – and another place in the Valley I don't go because of that?

Juniper pulls a face. 'Hold on, why would you even ask if she's going?'

Marlowe's gaze shifts off to the side of the screen, and I feel like she's weighing up how much she wants to drop me in it right now. If only she knew.

'Well ...' I say on her behalf. 'Kade and I are working together at the moment and, I guess you could say we've reached a certain kind of truce.'

Juniper stops walking and stares directly into the screen, people dodging around her – how busy is it where she is right now?

'Temperance Archer. Why?' She shakes her head. 'I have so many *why* questions about this, but the biggest one is WHY DO YOU LOOK LIKE THE CAT THAT ATE THE CANARY right now?'

She squints down at the phone and then bursts out laughing. Marlowe bites back her own smile, and heat races across my cheeks as they split into a grin. I bloody knew I wouldn't be able to keep a straight face about this. And I can't believe I'm about to say it out loud.

'Oh shit,' I confess, 'this is harder than I thought.' They both wait while I fumble with where to start. 'I'm ... kind of sleeping with him.'

Juniper's jaw drops. 'I'm actually speechless.'

Marlowe doesn't speak, but concern flits across her face, and my chest sinks a little.

'It's not Kade,' she says quietly, as if she knows exactly what I've picked up on. 'I like him – I really do, and I meant what I said about having your back. And honestly,

I like him for you. But his family, Peri. We just need to be ready.'

'I will kill that man before he hurts you, Peri,' Juniper declares. 'And I know people,' she warns.

I laugh at the fire in her tone, even if I can't quite shake Marlowe's comment. 'If you mean Beckett and his connections, I'm pretty sure the fact that he's a blood relative of Kade's will mean you're out of luck.'

'Rubbish,' Juniper counters. 'Kade *and* Beckett would probably thank me. Tell me, is he a good kisser? I've always thought that mouth would be—'

My whole face burns with something deeper than embarrassment, and I try to will it away. It's not a big deal. Just one of those things. We've been particularly busy doing *other* things.

'Oh, no kissing?' Juniper remarks, walking again, her attention divided. 'Just casual, then? Got it. I totally misread that for a sec. Although I would've thought you'd choose someone less complicated to scratch that itch. Is he good?' She looks at her phone and frowns. 'Damn, I have to take this. Don't share any juicy details without me. Love you both.'

She drops out of the call, leaving Marlowe and me staring at each other.

'I'm sure it doesn't mean anything,' Marlowe says quietly. 'The kissing thing. It's only new, right? But ... maybe you two should talk about what you're getting into. Make sure you really know the risks.'

I nod slowly. I'd thought we'd done that. But if he won't kiss me – which he hasn't – surely that can only mean he's not sure about it. About us.

I feed and check all the horses who are, thankfully, doing well. I know how quickly things can go bad with horses, and I never take their health for granted. The way my little foal frolics in the paddock before coming over to nuzzle at my hand never fails to lift my spirits, and I smile at her before letting my gaze drift to where the cottage sits. The cottage that used to belong to Riverbow and was – conveniently – removed when Walter Wilder had the council 'check' property borders.

The abandoned cottage that was going to be a holiday rental and then my grandfather's retirement home. I can't quite see it from here, but it has the best view of the river – a view I miss dearly.

Silently, I ask my grandfather if I'm doing the right thing. If these completely foreign feelings for Kade are worth the risk. But with no clear sign from him either way, I do the only thing I can think of and call my parents.

As I talk to them – minus many details, of course, and with a slight misdirection about Kade actually riding Nightshade and not just coaching Bree as my rider – my phone buzzes against my ear with a message.

'Peri, darling,' my mother says, 'we know you love that old farm. And we will do whatever we can to continue to support you with it. But at the end of the day, you can't let it stop you finding happiness. If Kade helps you with that, then we're here for that too. To be clear, neither your father nor I have anything against that boy. Honestly, he needs all the love he can get. His parents, rest their souls, would have given anything for those kids. His grandfather's sins are not his, remember that.'

As I hang up, feeling more conflicted than ever, I wonder how – if I lost Riverbow because of Walter Wilder – I could ever find happiness with his grandson anyway.

But still, as I read the message accompanying a picture of empty seating around an unlit fire pit, my pulse flutters, and I can't help but smile at the idea of seeing him again.

Kade: I think it's time we lit it up.

But I can't tell if he's just talking about the fire pit at Jamie's house, or this thing between us.

Chapter Thirty

KADE

Temperance is due at Jamie's any moment, and my nerves are just about shot. I'd asked her to come over a little earlier than everyone else so we could talk first.

I swallow.

Asking her how she feels about taking this thing public with our closest friends feels immense. Like it's the first step towards my grandfather officially knowing – and facing what he'll try to do to her stud. Not to mention how massive it feels in terms of declaring how I feel. But I've been working on the grandfather bit at least: talking about Nightshade with all my contacts, showing the riders of the Wilder Station horses the videos of him competing, and just generally trying to push his reputation as far as I can. And I'll keep doing it.

Really, Temperance needs more diversity in her stallions before she'll gain any real traction, but it's got to start somewhere.

As for tonight, I have no idea how to act with her around my friends. Part of me thinks it would be easier if she wanted to keep this a secret, draw a line we can't cross. But Cami has been asking a lot of questions about the time we're spending together in my gooseneck, and Jamie has a permanent fucking smirk, and … not touching her might be the hardest damn thing I've had to do. I don't even want to think about the prospect of someone else getting the idea she could be theirs instead of mine.

The knock at the back door ratchets up my heart rate.

Framed by the dying light of the sky, Temperance is a fucking vision. Her auburn hair is swept back into a high ponytail, pieces flying around her face, and a pink blush on her cheeks like she jogged here.

I reach for her hip immediately and pull her in. 'Hey, Sundance,' I murmur into her hair, the loose strands tickling my nose.

She softens into me and smiles like she can't help herself either, and it hits me that I could spend forever watching her smile. Especially this one that shyly lights up her face just for me.

'Hey,' she says back, tipping her face up to mine.

I kiss her soft cheek and pull back, just in time to catch something flash across her face – not fast enough to work out what. My palms tingle with anticipation and I clear my throat, shutting the door behind her and leading her into the kitchen I now share with Jamie on a permanent basis and, often, Cami.

'Drink?' I ask.

'Please.'

She settles onto one of the two barstools, and I have to force away the memory of her on a different barstool not so long ago. How in the world will I ever have her in my actual bar again? Maybe we could—

Shit, *focus*, Kade.

'Thanks for coming early,' I begin, sliding the gin and tonic across the bench to her, the wariness clear on her face. 'I – ah – I just wanted to check in on how you'd like this to go?'

She frowns. 'The fire pit?'

I can tell she's being obtuse; she must've thought about this the same as me.

'I'm pretty deft at the fire pit, smartass. I mean us. Do your friends know about us? Are you okay for mine to know too?'

Pressing my palms flat on the bench, I hope she can't tell how much feels like it's riding on what she says next.

'Well ... my friends know, sort of ... yes' – the flood of relief is immediate, my lips twitching, desperate to pull into a smile – 'so I guess it would be unfair not to tell yours.'

I frown a little. 'If you don't want them to know, they don't know, Temperance. How you feel about this is important to me.'

She stares at me a long time, and a weird shimmy starts low in my gut, like she's about to say something I don't want to hear.

'I think,' she starts, pausing. 'I think I don't know what "this" is.'

I swallow. I guess that's fair. 'What do you want it to be?'

She laughs. 'I want you to answer that first.'

Standing, I cross my arms over my chest and study her in return. A little voice tells me to back away before I get something broken I can't replace. But a louder, much more insistent voice is screaming that this is my shot. I down my drink – a favourite gin that really should be savoured – and round the bench to stand directly in front of her.

She spins on the stool and looks up at me through her lashes, and I know I'm an absolute goner for this girl.

'I want … to behave like our families never met. I want to take out an ad in the local newspaper that says "Temperance Archer belongs to Kade Wilder". I want you to never worry that my family will fuck yours over in any way ever again.'

Her face goes from bright to shadowed at my last words, and she hooks her two index fingers into my front belt loops.

'That sounds … incredible. If perhaps a little unachievable,' she whispers. 'Although I think people would assume we're getting engaged if you took out that ad.'

Right now, that thought is nowhere near as terrifying as it probably should be.

'But that's not our reality,' she finishes.

'We can make it our reality. He's been quiet, and hopefully my calling his bluff on the rides will keep him that way. We just need to secure you a good handful of services – Night's unproven, but his runs and the foals he'll produce will tip the scales. He's an incredible horse. And,' I continue, 'I know you're aware this stud of yours isn't going to blossom overnight, which is exactly why you've got the flower business as well. There's nothing he can do to affect that.'

'But—'

'Sundance, before you say anything more' – my heart slams in my chest, loud enough that it's almost all I can hear – 'I'm in this. I know it was unlikely. I know people will talk. I know ... fuck, I've already lost what I was trying to do with the Wilder horses. But I also know I've *never* looked at anyone like I look at you. Never *felt* like this about anyone. Ever since you walked into my storeroom, I knew you were going to take more than my fucking gin.'

She stares at me, mouth parted slightly, her eyes welling. I sweep a thumb across her cheekbone before cupping her face and stepping between her legs. My throat thickens. I press my other thumb gently to her luscious mouth as I bring my hand up—

'Hi, hi!' Cami calls as she comes in through the back door and into the kitchen. 'Oh, shit. Sorry – I – this is so *exciting*!' she squeals as I freeze in place.

'What's exciting?' Jamie asks as he steps in behind her. 'Oh.'

I can't see their faces from here, and I'm fucking thankful.

Dropping my forehead to Temperance's, I exhale. Still fucking desperate for the claiming kiss I was about to give her – one that's now going to have to wait.

'I meant what I said,' I whisper. 'But I'm sorry they now know without you really agreeing.'

Her chest rises and falls, and then she grabs both my wrists.

'Ummm ...' Cami says over the rustle of grocery bags, 'we can just leave these here.' She dumps them on the counter.

'Yeah, ah – I'll start the fire,' Jamie adds, clearing his throat.

'I'll help with food,' Temperance calls back, loudly enough for Cami to hear. How incredible would it be for the two most important women in my life to actually be friends?

Then she looks up at me, and the room seems to tilt at the depth in her expression.

'Okay,' she whispers.

'Okay what?' I ask.

She exhales a small, steadying breath. 'Temperance Archer and Kade Wilder. Let's see if we can survive your grandfather.'

Chapter Thirty-One

KADE

I leave Temperance in my bed at Jamie's with a kiss to her forehead and a scribbled note on the bedside table. She's sleeping so soundly I can't bear to wake her. I'll swing by her place on the way to Wilder Station to check her horses, but then there's something I need to do.

Her declaration last night, plus the way she nestled against me by the fire while our friends talked and laughed, opened something inside me I never could've predicted. Jamie has always been friends with Linden and Marlowe but, given our families' issues, that connection has never included Temperance or me. Until now. And I have a sudden sense of grief that we've missed out on so much time.

But if not for Juniper, Marlowe, and Night – and, I guess, the fall of her last rider – I have no doubt we never would've come this far.

My heart twinges in my chest as I make my way up the driveway of my old home. It still looks good, the groundskeeper would make sure of that. One of what should have been my horses trots along the fence line, following me up the last section of gravel road.

I know Brody and Tray will look after them – and I'll be able to check in from a distance – but it's still not quite the same as being their legitimate owner.

But I think of Sundance's skin on mine, and I know there's no other choice I can make.

His truck sits in the sun just in front of the stairs to the verandah that wraps around the house. A verandah that holds both good and tough memories. Sitting in the twilight with my parents; chasing Cami with a ... sparkler, I think it was; and saying goodbye to Jamie at the end of whatever we'd been doing together – he could only visit when my grandfather was occupied with something else. Okay, that one is bittersweet. I think Jamie always knew, or sensed, what he was leaving me to after my parents died, but he was also a sign of what I had waiting once I got through whatever rage was brewing in the house.

My throat thickens. Despite the size I have on him now, my grandfather will always be somehow bigger – more powerful – than me. And it feels far more apparent now than it did when I told Temperance we could face him.

Fuck. Why does this always have to be so hard?

The top timber step creaks, and I take a steadying breath before letting myself in.

I hear him laugh before I see him, and I know immediately where he is.

'Back with your tail between your legs so soon?' he calls from the ground-floor office. 'Want the horses back?'

Pressing my molars together, I take a breath. Another.

Then I take the final steps to the office doorway and stop there – neither in nor out, but not close enough for him to strike from behind the desk. I force myself not to look at the cane leaning against the wall.

'The opposite,' I reply. 'I'm telling you personally – this thing with Temperance is about to get bigger. Thought you'd want to hear it from me.'

My grandfather, his black button-up shirt pristine, places his pen down and sits back in the tall leather chair.

'Why, in fuck's name, would I want to hear that from you?' he asks, voice even.

I match it, refusing to let the little boy who cowered before this man show now. 'So you know it's the truth. She's a good thing, and I intend to keep her.'

He stares for a long moment, and I will myself not to fidget. He hates fidgeting.

'I cannot believe you're slumming yourself with that family,' he says, crossing his arms. 'She must be a god-damn tomcat in the sack.'

I point at him. 'Do not—'

'What?' he snaps. 'Tell you what a fucking idiot you're being? Is this really how childish you are – you'll go down with a sinking ship because of a fucking horse?'

I don't respond. I'm screaming inside to defend Temperance, but it won't help. He made up his mind about her – and her last name – a long, long time ago. Combatting his bias with my feelings will be like throwing petrol on a bonfire.

He shakes his head and leans forward.

'You do this, Kade, and I take you – and Camilla – out of the will.'

The bottom of my chest opens up and my heart seems to drop straight through it.

'You wouldn't,' I say, aware of the breathlessness in my voice. He needs *someone* to leave everything to.

'Fucking try me. You think you don't have cousins who'd benefit?'

Beckett, I think immediately. He wouldn't do that to me either – though someone will. Even if they think they're doing the right thing, trying not to lose the station altogether, Cami won't see a cent of what it's worth. I don't doubt her ability to make it on her own, but not giving her anything – despite the fact she suffered through this upbringing the same as me – just isn't right.

'What do you want?' I grind out.

'Leave this fucking dalliance with the Archer girl where it belongs – in the dust. Stop riding that goddamn horse of hers and do your job. There are horses out there' – he jabs a finger towards the window – 'that need working, and I expect you to do it. Don't, and I'll make sure Camilla doesn't pass her final assessments –her professor sits on plenty of the same boards as me – and she's written off. She'll have nothing but student loans, no degree, and no inheritance.'

My chest compresses like someone's got me in a wrestling hold and is squeezing tight. I stare at him, my mind scrambling to make sense of it. What this means for Cami. She'd hate it, but I can support her with the bar. I don't know how I'll pay her a proper salary and clear her debts right now, but we'd figure it out.

Because letting Temperance down in this way …

But this station was supposed to be Cami's too. The last place she has left of our parents.

Nausea builds in my gut, right where my anger is starting to fester.

'You'd do that to your granddaughter?' I ask.

His eyes narrow. 'Cami was never supposed to inherit this station. I have not spent the last several decades trying to turn you into a Wilder only for you to fuck it away with the trash.'

My ears ring. Did he just call Temperance – *my* Sundance – 'the trash'?

'I beg your fucking pardon?' I spit.

'For fuck's sake, Kade,' he snaps, dark brows slashing downwards. 'It's not a hard goddamn choice. Lose the girl and you secure your future and Camilla's. Choose your dick over your brain and neither of you get anything. I did *not* fight so hard for this station, for some idiot grandson I never wanted responsibility for, to let it all go to hell!'

He draws a steady breath even as I feel like I'm trembling on the spot. I knew he'd never be happy about Temperance. But stupidly, I thought that meant raging at me, hating on *me*. In all the years of getting to know his fists, I should've known that was never the only way he hurt me. I've been too wrapped up in Temperance, too focused on how it feels to be an 'us'. To hear her say 'okay' and wrap herself around me in front of our friends. To declare I'm hers too.

Too focused on all of that to consider I might be destroying Camilla's life in the process.

'That's the choice, Kade,' he says into my silence. 'Go back to your job on the station, prep my horses, and lose the girl. You do *not* support her pathetic stud, and you will *not* be seen with her. Ever.' The corners of his mouth pull downwards. 'Or I disown you both, and maybe I'll take down your watering hole just for good measure. I'm playing golf with the head of the health department next week.'

I'm numb as I walk back to the truck.

But I shouldn't be surprised. Part of me can't believe how stupid I was to think there would be any other reaction. I could live with him taking the horses, with him writing me off, even. But not Cami. Not failing her at the degree I was only able to pay for the first year of – the one that's supposed to give her options. Not destroying the bar I've built with Jamie. Not ... destroying two of the people I love most in this world.

I barely want to think it, but while he didn't say it, I also know harming Nightshade to get what he wants wouldn't be off the table either.

Chapter Thirty-Two

TEMPERANCE

Kade's quiet when he arrives with his gooseneck on the morning of Nightshade's final ride, and my stomach issues a low, swirling warning. The note he left me at Jameson's just said he had something to take care of and, until now, I wasn't worried about what that was. But he's likely just focused on today.

It's the last competition. If Kade and Night do well, even in one ride, we go to Nationals. I'll officially be offering a nationally competing horse as my first stud stallion. We've already agreed to split any prize money, and the list of things jostling for that grows longer every day. But there's a thrum of excitement riding along with it too.

Opportunity, I think suddenly as I watch Kade load Night onto the truck. His forearms flex as he manoeuvres around the horse and gently ushers him on, Night's footfalls almost thundering in the soft pre-dawn.

After this weekend, there will be nothing but opportunity.

The corners of my mouth tug up as Kade shuts the large trailer door. I step closer – right into his space, the one that now feels like it was made for me – something that makes my skin tingle. I stretch up and press a kiss to his stubbly cheek.

Immediately, he wraps his arms around me and pulls me tight, dropping his forehead to mine on a pained-sounding sigh.

I clear my throat. 'You know you've got this, right?' I ask quietly, my hands resting on his sides where I can feel his ribs expanding with breath.

He pushes back and looks me dead in the eye, the swirl in my stomach ratcheting up several notches.

'Sundance,' he says, just as quietly. 'I can't ride today. I—' He lets me go and steps back, running a hand down his face and over his beard.

I just stare at him.

Can't ride today?

The physical distance between us feels like a vacuum against my skin.

'I want to,' he rasps. 'I really fucking want to – I want—'

I tilt my head, heart pounding in my ears. I know what this is. Admittedly, I haven't been through one in a long time and – as a fissure seems to form between my collarbones, ready to snake down the front of my chest – I've never been in one with this much pain cresting.

He's breaking up with me.

Less than a day after we officially came out to our mutual friends.

Less than a day away before we were meant to qualify for Nationals. When Ted was going to confirm his booking with Nightshade – my very first one. The one that will get my stud on the map.

Less than a day after I let myself believe we could do this – take his grandfather on, together.

My eyes widen, almost faster than my understanding.

'What happened?' I ask.

'It's not me,' he says. 'I don't care what he does to me. But …'

'Cami,' I confirm, thinking of the only other person Kade would care enough about to cause the anguish on his face.

He nods, and my heart sinks. 'And Jamie.'

'How?' I breathe, the enormity of what he must be feeling pressing into me and forcing the cracking in my chest lower – down from my collarbones and through my sternum.

Deeper.

Kade links his fingers and cups the back of his head, elbows splayed out as he looks up at the sky – a move that's almost pure vulnerability. Vulnerability he's trying to hide from me.

I step into him again and he drops his hands. I grip them in mine between us and search his face.

'Tell me how,' I repeat.

I have to know if this is unavoidable. I've come so far with him, let him so far in I just …

My eyes burn. This is going to break parts of me I'm confident I'll never be able to repair. I need to know if there really is no other choice.

'Cami's lead professor – the one marking her final assessment – is on a board with Walter. I don't know what he has on him, but Walter's going to make him fail her.'

I bite the inside of my lip. I know teaching isn't Cami's passion but, from what I understand, she's done well in her degree, and to come away with nothing is vastly unfair.

'And he'll disinherit her, as well as me.'

Shit. 'So she'll have no qualification to show for her time, effort, or expense?'

Kade shakes his head.

My jaw feels tight. 'And neither of you have the station. Jamie?' I ask.

'He'll come after the bar.'

It's my turn to step back, my body too taut to be held close. That fucking asshole.

'That bar is you too, Kade. He's leaving you with no inheritance, none of your parents' legacy or what you've contributed to that place, and no way to earn an income on your own? The three of you will be, what, homeless?'

He purses his lips slightly, like he's running though scenarios in his head. Maybe homeless is a stretch – there's plenty of room here, after all. But even as warmth creeps over my skin at the thought, I know it's not the solution. They can't live here indefinitely. Not all of them.

They'd get jobs of some kind – they're smart, good, hardworking people – but in this town, those opportunities will be slim. Unless they each find a sudden passion for making coffee or picking flowers for free.

No, it's not that they'd be completely helpless or destitute. It's that Walter Wilder will have stripped them of the things that make them *them*. Things they've worked so hard for, that they're proud of, known for, and light up their souls.

Just like he did to my grandfather.

And it's because of me.

Tears prick my eyes, but I refuse to let them fall. I want to be strong for Kade. I need to be strong for me. Even I can't yet comprehend how I've managed to also be completely fucked over by a Wilder ... just like my grandfather was.

Was he also too naïve, too trusting, too ... whatever it is that's led us here?

It's stupid, really. I knew there'd be no good outcome from being involved with a Wilder. I just didn't expect to find so much good in one either. One I wanted to keep. One I—

My heart twists as I look at him, finding him watching me, shoulders dropped and hurt written all over his face.

'I've never been able to escape him, Sundance,' he murmurs. 'I can't let him take you or anyone else I love down with me.'

I roll my lips together, nose burning, forcing back the tears.

'I'm sorry,' he whispers, reaching for me and drawing himself around me. 'I'm so, so sorry.'

His words are soft in my hair but sharp in my chest.

It's clear we both know there's no way out of this.

Walter is powerful on the council. He can virtually run this town in any direction he chooses. Leaving Blackwood Valley gives him the same result as if we stayed. And leaving means we both lose our home too.

Where would we go, anyway?

My whole history is here, as is Kade's. That's not all good in his case, but his parents were here too. Jamie's here, and Cami clearly doesn't want to leave either.

I weave my arms around him tighter, sliding my hands up around his shoulder blades and turning into his neck. 'I'm sorry too,' I breathe against him.

Chapter Thirty-Three

TEMPERANCE

The drive to the showground is quiet.

Full of everything we haven't yet been able to do, or say to each other, and now never will.

I've wracked my mind for a way out of this the whole several hours' drive. But I'm not on the council and, even if I was, I'd never be as influential – or, likely, as manipulative – as Walter Wilder. So I can't protect Kade's bar. Nor do I know Cami's professor, so I can't work anything there either.

Even if I could, would I be successful?

And I'd be risking all of their – and my – futures for what? A brand new, untested thing with Kade?

I look out the window at the scenery flying past – the crops and fences and tall grasses at the side of the road. I wish it felt like I could let go of him as easily as the view slips by.

But he changed something in me, and now I wonder if anyone else would have ever been able to do that. Will ever be able to do that again.

I laugh, the slightly unhinged undertone clear even to me.

'You know you never even kissed me?' I throw into the truck cab.

Part of me immediately regrets it. What could he possibly say to that now? But it stings all the same, and some base part of me wants him to know. It's not because we were a casual hookup, like I worried after that call with June. If that was the case, it never would have come this far with his family. Knowing that doesn't mean I understand why, though.

'I know,' he says quietly, and I shift in my seat so I'm at least partly facing him, the seatbelt cutting across my chest and shoulder. 'I don't really … kiss people—'

I can't help the audible inhale at his words. Kiss *people*? Surely he doesn't mean—

'Like, you don't fully invest in your hookups, you mean?'

He cuts me a glare. 'Do *not* do that. You were not just a fucking "hookup" and you know it.'

And yet, he's already talking about me in the past tense.

Slowly, I turn back in my seat and look out the windscreen – at the road stretching ahead of us and the entry sign to the showgrounds on the left-hand side. I glance at him once more, soaking in his profile, but he says nothing more, and I can't bring myself to ask again.

Perhaps it's better I never know the answer to that particular question. I already know I'll never be enough in the face of everything he stands to lose because of me, and I don't want to be. I will never be the person who contributes to that. Who becomes like his grandfather.

At least I get to hold onto myself out of this. Even if that girl's heart is broken.

Kade pulls up in the large space near the stalls, and I unbuckle and slide out of the cab before he can say anything.

'Thanks for the ride,' I say just before I shut the door, my voice thicker than I'd like. 'I'll ask Bree and her boyfriend to pick us up.'

The door thuds shut and we look at each other for a long moment through the glass. I can only just make out his features through the tint, but they're overlaid with my reflection, and I painfully tuck that image away for another time.

Then I turn and unload Nightshade from the gooseneck, wondering what the fuck I'm going to do at this competition now that I have a horse and no rider.

No Kade.

My limbs are heavy as I lead Night to his allocated stall away from the mares and start to brush him down. I listen to Kade heft the saddle onto the rail, but I don't turn to look at him. Instead, I study the way the short brush bristles move along Night's muscled shoulder. How the dust from the trip makes little swirls in the air before being swept away.

Kade's footfalls dissipate quickly and—

'—right choice, son.'

My skin crawls at the voice I can just make out. I know if I turn now I'll see Walter Wilder, looking up at Kade – who stands taller than him – arrogance all over his face.

I want to scream when I do finally spin and find them halfway between here and the truck.

Kade is as still as a statue as Walter continues.

'—pleased you've seen the light and rid yourself of the trash.'

Alarm spikes through me as Kade steps forward, fists clenched, chin tipped at his grandfather.

'Kade!' I call out, heart hammering.

He didn't have to tell me repeatedly that he never wanted to be like him. Never wanted to use his hands or body to make people do things. I could feel it in my bones when he told me about his childhood, when he talks about Camilla, when he touches me. I watch him take a purposeful step back, hands still fisted at his sides.

Walter laughs, and acid burns my throat as he steps around Kade and smirks at me while he walks past.

'You're an unbelievable asshole,' I spit, and he smiles at me as he halts on the other side of the rail of Night's open-air stall.

'I'd beg your pardon,' he says, 'but you Archers have never had any manners.'

'Manners should be the least of your concerns when *this*' – I gesture to Kade – 'is how you'll be remembered.'

He leans forward, the harsh lines in his face and his ice-chip eyes full of vitriol. 'I will be remembered for making the hard fucking choices for the betterment of my bloodline and this town,' he snaps. 'I will be remembered for always coming out on top. And – unlike your sad, weepy grandfather – I will at least *be* remembered.'

He spins on his heel and strides off towards the arena, my impotent anger filling the stall as my ribs feel like they might explode.

I glance up in Kade's direction, where he's clearly been watching the whole exchange as if he was moments away from stepping in and has been reining himself in. Slowly, his fists start to relax. He holds my gaze for a long moment – one that feels very much like it's the last – and walks away.

I gear up Nightshade in a daze, still completely unsure what I'm going to do from here. It's our last qualifying run before Nationals. The one that was going to mean I could lock in the deal with Ted Carter and kick off Night's services – not to mention get some income I could reinvest in the stud and the ranch.

Thinking about how the inside of my chest feels carved raw is simply too much right now.

The voices of the other competitors drone around me as the loudspeaker crackles, and dust circles my boots while we walk towards the arena. Country music filters through the air, but this particular song isn't heartbreaking enough to match what's currently shattering within me.

Night nudges my shoulder with his nose and I try to smile. Try to soften my energy for him.

I have no choice but to ride him myself, even without advising the officials of the change in rider. Riding itself wouldn't worry me in the slightest if we were just checking fences or working to socialise Loki's foal. But this is *actual* reining and reined cow horse – to qualify for Nationals. Something I've never wished for, and therefore never worked towards – as a rider – in my whole life.

I'm a farmer. Not a reining competition rider. However much crossover there may be in skills, I've never honed mine for this purpose.

And yet, I'm now our only shot.

The announcer calls our ride as next and my stomach rolls. I walk Night to the warm-up arena opposite the competition one and take him through a few laps, along with a few of the manoeuvres I know will be expected, and desperately try to recall the pattern.

Another rider muscles into my space in the warm-up arena and I move away, working Night in slow circles up the other end. After I'm sure he's warm enough and I've gently loped him a few times, I head to the waiting bay as the announcer calls our run.

Nerves are a storm in my gut. But they're smothered by something heavy – something that's taken up room in my chest that I can barely breathe around. I make myself focus on the rider currently in the arena. Notice their stops. The lead changes in the middle. That could actually be a horse Kade trained – a Wilder Station horse. I shift in the saddle.

I'm going to look like a fucking fool out—

'Hey,' someone calls, gripping my calf, and I flinch. Night gives a shadow of the movement, and I stroke his neck as I take in Cami standing beside us.

My vision blurs and a couple of tears escape down my cheeks. Cami gives me a sad smile. 'Bloody hell,' she says, 'I'm so sorry you've been dragged through this.' She releases my leg and takes the rein closest to her. 'Hop off, Peri. I've got this.'

Chapter Thirty-Four

KADE

The blood drains from my face as I watch from the back of the stands while Cami instructs Temperance to dismount. In part, I'm relieved for Temperance. Relieved and grateful that Cami is taking the lead and helping her. Because right now, the spark seems to have gone out of my Sundance, and my ribs squeeze at the knowledge that I did that.

But as Temperance moves away from the waiting area, out of sight of the arena, Cami puts her foot in the stirrup and mounts Nightshade instead.

I curse under my breath.

Cami is about to make me watch not one, but two women I love be destroyed by the same man. There is no way he's going to let her get away with this.

Moving out of the stands, I'm blocked by an ageing man in a dark brown hat with a plaited white trim.

Ted Carter.

The same man who was going to put in an order for Night's services if he did well enough at this show and got to Nationals.

'Excuse me,' I mutter, desperately trying to hold on to my manners and not lift him by the shoulders to move him out of my way. Not that he's small enough for me to do that – and obviously I'm not going to shove him.

'Let her be, son.' My breath catches at the term and the respect with which he seems to use it. I look at him properly.

'Mr Carter, sir,' I say, searching his hazel eyes that brook no argument. 'I just need to get to my sister.'

He smiles gently. 'I know you think you do, Kade. But you need to let her run.' He slips his hands into his jean pockets and turns so we're side by side, both looking out over the arena. 'She's about to do a damn good thing out there. Will she win? Probably not – as far as I know, she's not a competition rider. But she knows enough from you, and she knows her way around a horse. And she's doing something for herself and for another.' He gives me a glance. 'Maybe more than one.'

I shake my head. 'That's not—'

'Not the issue, I know.'

My stomach knots – the same way it used to when I was a kid and was caught between wanting to tell someone about Walter and needing to defend him to save my own pride.

I clear my throat. 'Then you know I need to get down there before she sets foot in that arena.'

'It would be a hoof, but I get your meaning.'

I turn to stare at him and he almost smiles, the moment not light enough for him to actually laugh at his own silly joke.

'All the same, I disagree,' he continues. 'You need to let her run.'

I glance wildly around the stands, searching for another way down that won't make me look completely deranged as I leap over the seats.

'Ask yourself what's holding you back,' he presses. 'What's stopped you physically removing me – I'm pushing twice your age, it wouldn't be hard – and made you hesitate in your race to her?'

My heart pounds. 'You did. You blocked my path.'

He shakes his head. 'No, it wasn't that. Look at her.'

I twist back to where I can see Cami. Her head is held high as she sits on the shiny black stallion. He's calm beneath her despite the proximity to the other, unfamiliar horses.

'Up next, Night by Night We Walk,' the announcer drones, and I freeze. If Cami rides that horse, our grandfather will follow through with his threats against her – despite what I've done. Despite the fact that I folded to save her. Gave up Temperance to save her.

Cami leans forward and strokes Night's neck, and when she looks up, her face is split into a blinding grin.

Holy shit, she *wants* this.

'Right now,' Ted says, 'by not intervening, you're helping both of those women.' He turns back to me, but I keep my focus on Cami as she walks Night into the arena and comes to a stop in the middle. She nods to the judges and begins the run, my fingers starting to tremble.

She's really doing this. Going against Walter.

For Temperance.

For me.

'Your grandfather has always been a right asshole,' he adds. 'The two of you' – he gestures between me and the arena where Cami is delivering a large circle, Night's tail streaming behind him – 'can create your own legacy. Turn the Wilders into something you're proud of, not something you run from.'

I'm speechless as I watch the rest of Cami's run. It's not flawless, but it's damn good, and my pulse thunders as it becomes clearer and clearer she has a solid shot at making sure Night qualifies for Nationals.

She runs the final loop at the opposite end of the arena before charging down the long side and doing the longest stop I think I've ever seen Night do, one hand hanging on to her hat, and my chest explodes with pride. Cami makes her way back to the centre and gives the judges one last nod, her smile looking cemented on her face.

As she walks off the arena, the judges announce her score and the crowd erupts. She hasn't won, but perhaps more people here are like old man Carter beside me. Maybe more of them know the true nature of Walter Wilder than I'd realised.

Tentatively, I seek him out in the crowd. His face is a thundercloud, and it still makes my nerves skitter. But I look away and back to Cami, drawing on her obvious strength to steady my breath.

When she's almost at the arena gate, Cami spins Nightshade on the spot and looks up at me in the stands. She lifts her hat off her head and punches the air with it. The crowd cheers again. So loud they start to fade away as I focus on

Cami. On what she's done. Achieved all on her own. Then I copy her action until it feels like it's just the two of us in this space, hats held aloft.

Successful and defiant against Walter Wilder.

Chapter Thirty-Five

TEMPERANCE

The drive away from the arena and Nightshade's first run is like tearing off velcro that's stuck too hard. Unfortunately this time, as Jamie drives me home, leaving both Kade and Nightshade feels like it's tearing off bits of my skin.

Nightshade will be okay with Cami, and I text Bree not to come.

Kade will hopefully be the same – okay with Cami. It seems like such a waste to have taken Nightshade there only for him not to compete; I was barely even there for the first morning of the final competition. But I'm grateful to Cami for taking that choice from me. For leading him from the arena when I couldn't – we both knew I wasn't really going to be able to ride.

Still, the nausea hasn't abated since Kade told me what Walter is planning.

'Are you sure Cami knows what she's doing?' I ask Jamie, my voice flat.

His hands slip around the steering wheel a little as he flexes them. 'Yeah, she does,' he replies in what I've come to know as Jamie's typical quiet-but-strong tone. It's a voice with a calm authority to it.

'Does she know what Walter wanted to do?'

Jamie glances at me. 'Try to block her degree? She knows about that – and about not inheriting the station. But it's the bar that will worry her the most.'

I press the pads of two fingers between my brows and rub. Hard.

'That's no better, Jamie. I can't have destroyed not only something that you love, but something you earn an income from.' I swallow. 'I know how hard it is to eke out a living here. I would never wish that on you all.'

'We'll be fine,' he says. 'There are other places Cami can finish her degree if she has to. Places outside the Wilder influence – he doesn't run the country, after all, just the county. As for the bar' – he shrugs a shoulder – 'we'll be able to ride out whatever comes our way.'

I press my hands between my knees. 'How can you sound so calm?' I ask.

He seems to give that some consideration, and I glance at him. His dark brows are furrowed slightly, dark brown hair falling over his forehead. He's handsome in an *I'm dark and broody* kind of way. Not like Kade, who is all rough edges and blond beard and piercing blue—

I push away the vision of his face.

'Because on this side, it's more about the challenge of Cami and Kade facing him – their grandfather. The future of Wilder Station aside, he doesn't have as much influence over their choices as he claims.' He throws me a look, and I catch the worry there. 'You, though,' he continues, 'you're operating directly in his sphere of influence, and he's been in that space a long, long time. His view still counts for a lot with those folks.'

I nod. He's right, and the enormity of him saying it out loud makes me drop my head into my hands.

'Do your parents know?' he asks, and I sit up again.

'About me and Kade?'

'And what Walter has threatened – to ruin you before you even start.'

'Sort of … I wasn't entirely sure how that would go down. I've been a bit vague with them about how much Kade is involved – they think he's coaching Bree. As far as they know, it's a one-step removed kind of relationship with him and Night and me. Although, to be fair, I'm confident it would be different to Walter's reaction. But would they be supportive of Kade and me together?' I'm quiet for a moment. 'I don't know,' I admit. 'Walter essentially ran them out of town because they couldn't keep raising me here with no jobs and not enough income on Grandad's ranch to support us all.'

'I think you should give them a call,' Jamie says. 'At his core, Walter's a nasty fucking bully. You don't have to face that on your own.'

My fingers tremble a little when I hit 'call' on my phone as soon as Jamie leaves my driveway. In a way, I don't know why I'm nervous – Mum and Dad have never judged my decisions. At least, not in a mean way. They've always wanted what's best for me. Did they try to talk me out of taking on Riverbow? Yes. Did they want me to leave Blackwood Valley and find something else? Yes. Did they also want me to find someone who made me laugh? Also yes.

But have I done any of those things?

No.

Well, *yes* and no.

'Hi, pumpkin,' my dad greets after the fifth ring, and I try to smile. 'Hang on, I'll get your mother.'

He shouts down the house they now live in at Lake Wildes. I listen to what sounds like the phone being dropped between couch cushions before being retrieved, and then their peering faces appear on the small screen.

'Temperance,' my mother says, her voice full of so much warmth it makes my eyes sting. She frowns immediately. 'You look drawn, are you okay? Wait, I need my glasses.'

She disappears, and I use the few seconds of looking at their ceiling to compose myself.

Dad pushes himself back into the frame. 'She's not drawn, Lydia, she's exhausted. How was the show, pumpkin?'

My pulse kicks up a little and I sit forward, holding the phone between my knees. Reining – or anything competition-related in the horse world – was something my parents left behind when they moved from the valley. My dad was a particularly good rider at one point, but all farm work. Nothing he ever felt called to compete in.

'Yeah,' I mutter. 'That's kind of what I wanted to tell you.'

Mum's frown deepens, the crease between her brows clear. 'I knew something was wrong.'

I sigh. 'Look, I'm probably both drawn and exhausted.' *And heartbroken*, I add silently. 'I wasn't totally honest with you. Bree wasn't riding Night. She hasn't since the start of the season—'

'Why?' Dad interjects.

'She came off one of her own, like I told you, but she busted her leg. She's fine,' I hasten to add.

'Oh.' Mum sucks in a breath. 'Poor Bree. But I don't understand – how, why didn't—'

'I partnered with Kade Wilder,' I explain. 'He rode Night in the first two qualifiers and ... his sister Cami took him round this last one.'

My heart sinks further into my gut. I don't even know how they went. The weight of my own cloud so heavy, I haven't checked in to see how Nightshade or Cami are. Cami, I'm not sure I can bring myself to talk to after embarrassing myself so thoroughly she had to take pity on me. As for Night, I should've been there for him. I know he's in good hands, but he's still mine. And I just left him there.

'*The* Kade Wilder?' Dad asks. 'The boy you swore you'd hate forever? You let him do more than coach Bree? He rode Nightshade?'

Now it's my turn to frown. 'I didn't swear to hate *him* forever. I swore to hate the Wilders forever.'

'I feel like that's splitting hairs,' he says.

'And I distinctly remember the first birthday party where you realised everyone in your year was invited except you, and you promised you'd never forgive him,' Mum adds. The corners of her mouth kick up. 'But maybe you took my advice and forgave him a little?'

I shake my head as I try to calibrate everything running through me. I wish there was something about this that was funny.

'I loathe that man,' Mum mutters about Walter after I've finished filling them in – telling them all the ways he would've ruined us if this weekend hadn't gone the way it did. Although ... does he know Cami took Night from me at the arena? What did he make of that? He was probably pleased to see how defeated I was.

'Temperance,' Dad says, his dark eyes hard. 'Your grandfather backed down from Walter, and he still lost his spirit. That, more than anything, ruined him. Walter screwed him with the purchase of that horse, it's true. But then he didn't fight back. Walter reworking the boundary to cut out the cottage was just because he could – just so he could kick Dad while he was down.'

The back of my nose burns. The change was subtle at first. So subtle I barely noticed anything was wrong. But maybe that was because I was young. Perhaps also because he tried to hide it from me. And then, one day, it seemed to be all he could talk about. His shoulders drooped as he'd stare out at the view from the back porch. Tell me about everything he'd lost and could never make right.

'Don't be like him,' Mum murmurs. 'If you and Kade think you have something, fight for it. Honestly, darling,

Walter could come for you whether you and Kade are together or not. You might as well have something good in your life while he does.'

I stare at her. 'I don't know if that's supposed to be uplifting or not.'

She pulls a face. 'Just real, darling. But above everything else, you don't let that man take your fighting spirit.'

Chapter Thirty-Six

KADE

Dust kicks up around my truck as I screech to a halt behind Cami's on Temperance's ranch. She hasn't unloaded Night yet, and I force hard breaths in and out through my nose. She refused to answer my calls the whole drive here, and it's done nothing to ease the herd of elephants rampaging through me.

What the *fuck* was she thinking?

Walter is going to destroy her future. A future I worked really fucking hard to make sure she had. The elation of the moment has well and truly gone; the assurance and comfort Ted Carter gave me has dissipated like I imagined that whole exchange. Now I just feel panic gripping my veins. That I managed to stay long enough after the run to know she'd qualified is a miracle in itself. But it was a relief to know we didn't have to complete any other runs to get the scores needed for Nationals, despite the huge problem that also presents. Because who the fuck is going to ride there? Bree? Has she healed?

I sit in my truck, fuming, as Cami backs Night off her float and then looks at me with a 'now what?' expression.

Obviously she's never been on the Archers' ranch before. Growing up on the land next door doesn't mean much when you're miles away from each other. Particularly when contact was essentially banned.

Gritting my teeth and moving slower than feels natural right now, I get out and softly close my truck door.

'Over there,' I say, pointing to the yard I work him in. I can see the gate is open to the paddock beyond.

Temperance's truck is where she normally parks it, alongside the house. But whether she's in there, I don't know – we didn't take it to the show. My heart hammers. Did Jamie bring her back here, or did she want to be taken somewhere else?

I run my gaze over the windows of her old house but see no movement. Is she hiding from me?

What would I say to her after today, anyway? After I left her.

Before Camilla swooped in and saved the day.

My blood feels like it's curdling. How was my little sister brave enough – strong enough – to do what I couldn't?

The memory of waking up with Temperance, in the house I'm currently staring at, slams into me like I've been backed over by my gooseneck. How is it real that I'll never—

Why did I not kiss her properly? Not give her everything in that way too?

Why would I hold back from her?

Because it's now abundantly clear she has everything of me anyway. I'm walking away not knowing what it feels like to have her lips on mine.

My chest is tight, and I bring my focus back to my breath – something I've done thousands of times in my life but never like this.

Ten, I take a mental step back from the image of Temperance's hair strewn across the pillow.

Nine, I let the feel of her fingers on my ribs trail away.

Eight, the look in her eyes when she knew we'd have to end—

My breaths are too fast, and I step back towards my truck, blinking into the darkening sky.

Fuck. I lost her to save Cami and Jamie, and Cami just threw it all away anyway. I can only imagine what my grandfather is planning right now. Has he already made the call to Cami's professor? Has she already lost her escape from Blackwood Valley?

And I've shown Temperance that I can't, won't fight—

The bar. I need to—

'Kade.' Cami's voice is sharp as I wrap my fingers around the door handle of my truck.

I go still, staring at my dim reflection in the driver-side window. My eyes are hidden in shadow. I can see the heaving of my chest in the glass, and I shut my eyes. Slow my breaths.

But I still can't turn around.

'Kade,' Cami says again from behind me. 'Count them.'

I grit my teeth. I hate that she knows this part of me so well. I'm supposed to be her protector, but I lost count of how many times she sat with me through an attack a long time ago. She never asked where they came from, and I never offered. But watching her throw her ride in Walter's face today ... perhaps she always knew what I was shielding her from.

Perhaps that was also her way of saying *enough is enough*.

'Ten,' she murmurs as I exhale, clearly watching my body.

I bow my head and suck oxygen through my nose and into my belly as Cami counts my exhales.

Her voice washes over me, and I let myself notice how my pulse slows. Steadies.

She stays silent for a long time after we get to 'one', and Riverbow Ranch is almost completely dark around us. No lights are on when I finally open my eyes and search the house, my stomach sinking.

Clearing my throat, I turn to Cami and nod.

'You okay to drive?'

'Yeah,' I reply.

'Let's talk at Jamie's.'

'He's a fucking asshole, man,' Jamie mutters as we sit around the fire pit in the late summer evening – thankfully now past fire-ban time. 'But we've always known that. This is just the final cutting of the cord, and I get that's ... complicated. Painful, even. But' – he glances between the two of us – 'you'll both be better off without him.'

'Without the station?' I ask, wondering if Jamie really understands how much that legacy means to me, and what the station can do for our financial security.

'Yes, Kade,' he replies gently, 'without the station. You know you can support yourself well enough with the bar, and—' He looks at Cami as if handing over to her.

I shake my head. I know what's coming.

'I can support myself, Kade,' she murmurs, before reaching out and placing her hand on my knee. 'Mum and Dad are gone. I may not remember much of them, but I simply cannot bring myself to believe this is what they'd want for you. There's nothing there for us to hold on to anymore. This is not the legacy we want.'

I sit back in the old camp chair and look up at the sky, not enough energy to even curse.

'And how will you support yourself with no degree, Cami?' I ask.

They're both silent long enough for me to know they've talked about this in advance.

'The bar can take her on,' Jamie says, 'and we—'

'No,' I cut in, pinning him with a glare. 'Not a fucking chance. I want her out of this town. *Options.* She needs fucking options, and working for us with no out isn't enough.'

Jamie's features fill with resignation. I hadn't realised how much he might want Cami at the bar. She'd be an absolute asset – I know that – but that's not the point.

'And if he takes down the bar too?' I press. I need them to understand how much more I need for Cami.

The three of us watch the fire for a long time, the air heavy with everything we haven't said yet.

'You need to go after Peri,' Cami says eventually, and she may as well have struck me in the ribs.

I laugh, but it's bitter even to my own ears.

'Cami, I love you,' I say, 'but you're not getting this. He will *ruin* us if I do that. I cut all ties with Temperance, train his horses, and one day we get the station. We deserve that station – it's supposed to be ours. I will work it, save our money, build the bar, and *you* get to live your life, Cami.' My voice starts to strangle. 'That's all I want. I just – I just need you both to live your lives.'

I don't say I have no fucking idea what's going to happen now that she's ridden Nightshade.

Cami leaves her chair and drops to her knees in front of me, taking my hands in hers. 'No, Kade, it's *you* who's not getting it. Why do I get to have a life and you don't? Why am I more deserving of that than you?'

'Because' – my fucking eyes start to burn – 'I need to know I did *one* fucking thing right.'

'Damn it,' she chokes out, tears glistening on her cheeks as she shuffles closer. 'You have done so much right. But don't lie to me, or to yourself. You want more with Peri – I know you do. And you deserve that too.'

'No—'

'*Listen* to me, you stubborn ass.' Her voice wavers but doesn't break. 'He can try to fail me, but I can transfer and finish my study at another uni. Or report any professor who might unfairly try to fail me, be assessed by someone else – there are processes for this stuff, Kade. And do you really think I'm at the only higher education institute in the country? As for the bar, the worst he can do is agitate the council to make life hard, whisper things to his friends who are too senior to want to get into that detail. But every other member of the council loves your gorgeous bloody bar, and your gin, and what it does for tourism – it's not going anywhere.'

'I need you to promise you'll go,' I murmur. 'Leave the valley.'

She stares at me for a long beat, and Jamie seems as still as I am. Then she nods. 'I promise.'

I feel like the fire is spinning around us, Jamie silently watching on, as I search Cami's face. 'And the station? Our history? You'd walk away from all of that?'

'I already have,' she breathes. 'You're all I have left of my family, and I need you to have a life too. Fuck that toxic legacy, Kade. Let's make our own.'

Chapter Thirty-Seven

TEMPERANCE

Juniper's face is flushed with anger when I finish telling her and Marlowe what happened with Kade. 'How dare that old bastard,' Juniper fumes. 'I'm so sad for you, hun, and I'm so mad on Kade's behalf. Expectations you don't ... doesn't matter. That old man should rot as far as I'm concerned.'

'You really love him, don't you?' Marlowe asks, her brows furrowed.

A tear slips from my eye and slowly tracks its way towards my pillow. Another tickles over the bridge of my nose. 'If love is this painful, I don't want it.'

'Well,' June says, 'I'd say Marlowe is the best of us to answer that. Last I heard things were still going well with Henry. But me? Not a clue what love is supposed to be.'

'I think ...' Marlowe offers, 'you need time. Both of you. For you, time to grieve it and allow yourself to move on. I really like Kade, but his demons with his grandfather aren't yours to slay. For him, I think he needs time to work through what his next steps are. I can't imagine growing up with ... that.'

'You mean our short time together isn't enough to make him blow up his whole life?' I try to joke, but it falls flat. Kade's desire to protect Cami and Jamie – and me – has just made me love him more.

My phone pings with an email notification. One to my stud email that's existed in echoing online silence.

I sit up and wipe my cheeks. *Shit.* Maybe it's Mr Carter officially telling me his interest in Night is over.

'Peri, what's up?' June asks, but I'm no longer looking at her as I navigate to my email app. 'I think I just went on a virtual emotional roller coaster.'

'I just—' I scan the inbox. 'Theodore Carter' sits in the 'from' field, and I want to be sick. 'I got an email.'

'Ah, okay …' Juniper says cautiously.

'Open it while we're here,' Marlowe urges. 'You're worrying me.'

I swallow. 'It's probably nothing more than expected – my stud isn't going to get off the ground.'

'Open it,' Marlowe repeats gently.

'I'd just delete it, so yes, better listen to the sensible one just in case,' June adds.

Holding my breath, I open the email. I scan it quickly, then go back to the beginning. 'Holy shit,' I whisper.

'What is it?'

'Tell us!' Juniper yells over Marlowe.

'It's Mr Carter,' I breathe. 'He wants to book a service with Nightshade.'

'That's fantastic,' Marlowe says while Juniper squeals.

'I can't believe it,' I murmur, bringing them back on the screen and trying to work my mind around what this means for me – and how Kade and Cami might be paying for it.

'Believe what?' Juniper asks. 'That you're like a horse pimp now? Me neither.'

I laugh and sniff at the same time. 'Maybe that could be a new song for you.'

'Yes! I'll get Linden to write it for me.'

After reading the short note out loud to them both so we're absolutely sure, I say goodbye to June and Marlowe so I can wrap my mind around the email and respond to Ted about next steps.

Then I stare at my phone.

I just got my first booking for Night, and I'm burning with the need to tell Kade. And yet – how do I tell him that our risk was good for me and cost him everything, not to mention it put Cami at risk too?

I do my late afternoon check, feeding and rugging the horses, and give Night an extra treat. How amazing that he has no clue how integral he is to my future and to rebuilding my grandad's legacy. He huffs a low breath that flaps his lips as I stroke his nose, and I can't help giving him a watery smile.

Gazing out across the paddocks towards the river I can't quite see from here, I feel the pull to visit the old cottage. The one my grandad loved so much he proposed to my nana in it. The one Walter Wilder took away – and broke my grandad's spirit doing so.

The walk isn't long, maybe fifteen minutes from the main house, but the cottage feels like a world away. Tucked in a little cleared patch of land surrounded by willows with a front-row seat to the bend in the river, it's a breath of fresh air.

It needs a new life, and it still angers me that Walter stripped us of it just to let it rot, but here we are. The fence my grandad had to erect to show our new boundary doesn't even get maintained. Like Walter only cared about making sure we didn't own it – not about the cottage itself.

I gingerly test the narrow steps that lead into the house and – assessing the worn wood with a few flakes of what was once white paint as strong enough to sit on – sink down and face the river. It gurgles and bubbles around the bend, and I try to let the sound soothe me.

But there's a wound under my skin like I've never experienced before. And it's festering with worry about Kade. I know he didn't want this. Didn't want to let go of whatever we were building, but he had no choice.

Fresh tears prick my eyes. He never kissed me. Does that mean he didn't fall for me the way I fell for him?

I send Juniper a silent thank you for not raising that on our call. For not questioning how I could've let myself fall for someone who didn't feel enough for me to even put his mouth on mine.

Mum told me not to lose my fighting spirit, but as I sit on the front steps of the old cottage my grandad wanted to restore, I wonder if I ever really had enough fight to go against Walter.

Not knowing if I'm making a terrible decision, I take a photo of the riverbank and send it to Kade with a '?'. It's the same place he has a photo of in his bar, but I can't be sure he'll recognise it.

Heart hammering, I make myself put the phone down and wait.

In less than two minutes, it buzzes – and I open the message.

It's a short clip of Kade turning the ignition in his truck.

Chapter Thirty-Eight

KADE

My breathing is harder than it should be, but in a different way than the last time I was here. When Cami had to count me down.

Has Temperance opened the door to us? Even though I let her down in a terrible, terrible way? Or is she working herself up to tell me how much of an asshole I really am – how much of a *Wilder* she thinks I really am.

Either way, the need to see her coursing through my veins had me in that truck before I could even tell Jamie and Cami where I was going. I feel bolstered by the conversation I had with them around the fire. I hadn't realised how much I needed their permission to let go of my grandfather and everything he represents. To let go of the station, even though it's painful. How much I needed their assurances that it's not all on me to keep all our heads above water.

I leap out when I reach Sundance's ranch, grabbing the torch from my glovebox just in case, and all but run towards the cottage. I've never been there from this side, but I know exactly where it is.

It's dark enough that I have to slow as I reach the old fence, easily stepping through and letting the wire sag behind me. The cottage looms like an ink-coloured shadow just to my right, and I let my eyes continue to adjust.

And she's there.

Sitting on the step like she's been waiting for me her whole life.

My heart twists in my throat.

'Hey,' she says quietly, prompting me to keep walking. 'I'm pleased you came.'

I almost stumble. Is that how she'd start a breakup speech? But I guess we're already broken up. If we were ever really together.

I want to shake myself. She's here. I'm here. Cami and Jamie are okay. We're going to figure this out.

'You called, I came.'

She looks up and tilts her head at me as I approach. 'I didn't call.'

'No,' I concede as I drop down beside her. 'But you wanted me – I think – so, close enough. I'm here.'

She looks towards the black river. 'I wanted you,' she murmurs, before turning to me and flaying me open with a look.

Her green eyes are almost the shade of darkest moss in this light, but the dying day doesn't take the edge off their intensity.

'I want you, Kade,' she continues, sucking the air from my chest. 'I want Cami and Jamie to be okay, and I want to help make that happen, but I don't want to have to lose you in the process. I think we have something here worth fighting for and—'

I crash my mouth to hers.

It's not pretty. It's desperate.

And it seeps into all my fissures.

Temperance whimpers into me, a sound that whips right through the centre of my chest.

Her lips are soft – softer against mine that I could've ever imagined – and then she drags her teeth over my bottom lip. She presses closer, pushing me back on the step and moving to straddle me.

I find her tongue with mine as I wrap my arms around her and grip her ass, helping her grind on me, the pressure creating black spots at the edge of my vision.

'Wait,' I gasp, breaking the kiss and tucking a strand of hair behind her ear.

She frowns a little, and I smile. She's both intrigued and desperate for me, and it's a heady feeling.

'I'm sorry,' I say, not realising how important it was to get that out before things go further. 'I never should've left you like that.' A wash of shame weighs down my shoulders.

Temperance takes my face in her hands. 'Kade, you made a stand for your family. I admire that, I really do.'

'But I hurt you in the process.'

She sighs. 'Yes, I was hurt. But I also recognise the impossible situation you were in and we – well, I don't know – but you love Cami and Jamie, and I respect that you look after those you love.'

Her gaze bores into me, and I need her to keep talk-ing. My whole body tingles with what I want her to feel for me.

I let my hands run over her ass, slow and reverent, memorising the curve of it and how perfectly she fits in my lap. 'Still,' I whisper, 'I wish I hadn't done that. At the same time, if I hadn't, Cami wouldn't have run the hell out of Night.'

She sits back, hands on my shoulders. 'What do you mean?'

I grin. 'She smashed it.'

My Sundance's mouth parts. 'You mean—'

'We qualified for Nationals. The four of us.'

She laughs. 'The four of us. Holy shit. But what about Walter? I want to help—'

I pull her back in a little. 'You already have. If it weren't for you, I never would've had an opportunity to ride, to ... get to know you. And' – I huff a small laugh – 'I probably should've given Jamie and Cami more credit for having my back.'

'I have your back too, okay?'

I nod, my chest swelling several sizes.

'So,' she says, her face turning serious, 'I do need to know – much as I want to make this work, to ... see it through – if this is just for shits and giggles for you, I don't—'

I clamp a hand gently over her mouth. 'Don't you fucking dare keep suggesting this is for "shits and gig-gles". Do I really seem like someone who does "shits and giggles", Temperance?'

I keep my hand there until she shakes her head, and even then I wait another beat to be sure it's sunk in. Then I move my hand to cup the back of her head.

'Temperance Archer, I am so fucking in love with you it's almost madness. I'm choosing to leave behind what I thought I needed to do for Cami. And I'm going to look after her and Jamie – and you – in the way that's right for me.'

Her smile lights up the night, and my heart feels tied to a helium balloon. 'I want you to make love to me right here, Kade Wilder.'

I don't know if she realises it, but her saying my name hits me hard – drags me even deeper. Despite everything another Wilder has done, she says my name without shame. And she gives me permission to do the same.

This time, when Temperance kisses me, it's slow and warm, and I want to sink into it and never leave.

She trails kisses down my neck before unbuttoning my shirt and tugging it free. I watch her admire my chest and stomach, the hunger in her face making me harder. I rock up into her and the corners of her mouth tip up. Slowly, she pulls off her shirt, then her bra, and I watch her breasts settle with their own weight, practically begging me to take them in my mouth.

Temperance arches her back, inviting me to do just that, her moans like a drug as I bite each nipple and suck hard. She grips my shoulders and leans back, her breasts in my face, rocking against my cock.

She's fucking magnificent like this – uninhibited against the navy sky. Biting her lip, head thrown back. Just as I think I might blow in my pants, Sundance sits up and undoes my belt. I lift my hips as she drags my jeans down.

I fist myself slowly as I watch her stand and shed the rest of her clothes, then straddle me again, holding herself just above my cock – so close I can feel the heat of her.

'I love you too, Kade,' she breathes, sinking onto me in one smooth movement.

I curse, dropping to my elbows and thrusting up into her. Watching her tits bounce, I let her set the pace. Pressure builds beneath my balls and at the base of my spine as she rides me towards her own edge. Her breaths break in short pants and she cups her breasts – one in each hand – and I grit my teeth to hang on.

She braces a hand on my lower belly, broken sounds catching in her throat. 'I'm on birth control,' she gasps. 'Please, Kade, don't stop.'

'Take what you need, Sundance,' I rasp, driving up to meet her rhythm. Her pussy clamps around me, and then she shudders, calling out into the open night, milking my cock.

My climax tears through me, shaking my limbs. I clutch her to me as I spill into her, again and again.

We stay tangled together on the steps of the rundown cottage until the air turns crisp. I'm grateful I brought the torch, but a pang of loss still hits when she finally eases off me and tucks herself under my arm.

'I want to bury myself inside you every day,' I murmur.

'Okay,' she says simply, and I smile.

'Do you think that makes this cottage ours now?'

She turns to me, serious. 'You'd want that?'

'I want everything,' I breathe, pressing a kiss to her lips. She smiles against me. 'Then let's make it ours.'

Epilogue: Temperance

Meadow and Velvet is empty apart from our table, the country music drifting from the speakers filling the space around us.

'Well,' Juniper says from the screen of my phone, currently propped against the water bottle at the edge of the table. 'Here's to making it to Nationals!'

She holds up a cup of what I assume is coffee, given the time difference wherever she is, and the rest of us cheers with our respective drinks. Mine is one of my favourites of Kade's gins. The one that makes me think of barstools. I take a sip and cover my face with my hand, my cheeks aching from smiling. Next to me, Kade nudges his hand higher up my thigh, the warmth of his skin seeping through my jeans as he leans in.

'What is that face for?' he whispers, his breath tickling my cheek.

I glance at him, dropping my hand and looping my fingers through his over my leg. 'Take me to the storeroom later, and I'll tell you,' I murmur.

He barks out a laugh that has everyone looking at us, and Juniper cuts in, her mock glare filling the screen. 'Listen.

273

We can't all be that sickeningly loved up, so cut it out. I'm trying to—'

'Oh, Junie,' Linden says, glancing over at Coco playing in the far corner of the room with her favourite blue truck, 'let them have it.'

Juniper rolls her eyes. 'Marlowe, help!'

'She can't help you,' I reply, laughing. 'She's just got back from seeing Henry.'

There's a pause – a beat too long – and Marlowe's neck flushes as she waves us off. 'Oh, I'm not sure that's true,' she counters. 'I've been with Henry for two years, and we've never been like that.'

She raises a brow at Kade and me, and I exchange a pointed look with Juniper on the phone.

Marlowe and Henry needs some unpacking.

'Anyway,' Marlowe says, raising her glass again, 'seriously, congratulations to you all, and here's to making new friends, a pretty fabulous horse, and putting aside old murder wishes.'

'For now!' I call out.

Kade squeezes my leg, making me jump, and I squeal.

Cami catches my eye and smiles warmly, one I can't help but return. If it wasn't for her, none of us would've made it this far. None of us mentions the fact that we don't really know what Walter's next move will be. Has he already interfered with Cami's studies? What will she discover when she goes back to campus? Or will he come for the bar?

Either way, knowing he could still impact all of our lives – and not for the better – is a constant, low hum under my skin. But as I take in the people around me, and the weight of Kade's hand on my leg, I also know I wouldn't trade this for anything.

I dare Walter to try to take it from us.

'You'll come to Nationals?' I ask Cami, letting the congratulations and my thoughts about Walter fall away, and returning to normal conversation. In the background, I hear Juniper ask to talk to Coco, and Linden walks the phone over to her, crouching as the three of them laugh about something.

Cami looks between Kade and Jamie. 'I'd love to, but it'll depend on where I am. I have to go back to the city to complete my study next week and then ...' She shrugs.

'And then,' Kade says with a smile, 'the world is literally your oyster. No more Blackwood Valley.'

His voice is so full of pride it catches in my chest and starts to warm. But something in Cami's expression tells me she doesn't actually want *the world*. At the same time, it's clear how desperately Kade is hanging on to that option.

Jamie clears his throat. 'Anyone want another?'

He takes the various orders before heading to the bar, leaving the rest of us to keep talking. And Cami watching him. I narrow my eyes at her across the table, but she just blushes when she catches me and looks away.

'Maybe you need Cami to ride one of the others,' Linden suggests as he returns to the table and hands me my phone, Juniper having gone.

I stare at him for a moment, and he meets my gaze with panic in his eyes. It takes me a second to work out why my mind has stalled – and why he looks so guilty. Not so long ago, I would've wanted to kill him for letting slip to the Wilders about my secret horses. Now, I'm just disappointed I didn't get to show Kade Loki myself before now.

Kade cocks his head at me. 'Another horse?'

A slow smile spreads across my face. 'Well ... I can't really have a "stud" with only one stallion.'

He leans back, grinning, and runs a hand down his blond beard. 'Temperance Archer, what other secrets are you keeping from me?'

Laughing, I sit back in my seat and mirror his pose. 'Time will tell, Mr Wilder. Time will tell.'

As the words leave my mouth, a sense of wholeness washes over me because the truth is, there are no secrets from Kade. Just things to learn about each other.

Kade pushes his chair back and stands, placing a hand on my shoulder before sliding his fingertips up into my hairline. The sensation is like a waterfall of tingles from the crown of my head down to the apex of my thighs.

'Right,' he says, 'I'd better stock the bar. Thanks, everyone, for coming. It's ... actually really nice to have us all together like this.'

Marlowe and Linden share a look.

'Mate,' Linden remarks, swishing his dark brown hair off his forehead, 'if you and Peri had sorted your-selves out years ago, we would've been along for the ride. Do either of you know how painful it was to keep the friendship groups from crossing over?'

Kade squeezes the back of my neck, and my scalp prickles. 'Yeah,' he replies, 'you might have to take that one up with Temperance.'

I turn to watch him go, admiring his perfect ass in those jeans as he walks away.

'I can't tell you how good it is to see him so happy, Peri,' Cami murmurs, and my heart swells.

'I'm pretty sure that's not just me,' I admit, hoping she understands I also mean how she helped him stand up to their grandfather. How she gave the ride of her life and got Nightshade to qualify for Nationals. I regret not staying to see it – the replay was incredible, but I know it won't have been a patch on the real thing.

At the same time, I'm pleased it was something she and Kade got to share in front of Walter.

She gives me a shy sort of smile, and my phone buzzes on the table in front of me, the rest of the room fading away as a gentle hum fills my body.

Kade has sent me a photo of the storeroom.

Before you go

Want one more scene with them?

If you're lingering here because you're not quite ready to let them go yet ... or want to know what happened after that text ... I understand.

I wrote an **exclusive bonus epilogue** for readers who wanted to see what happens *after* the ending—when the storeroom door closes.

It's a delicious full circle moment. And you won't find it anywhere else.

Unlock the exclusive bonus epilogue.
Join my private reader list and I'll send it straight to you.

READ THE EXCLUSIVE EPILOGUE: https://la urenparkerrhodes.myflodesk.com/ggbonusepilogue
By signing up, you'll also receive early access to new releases, bonus scenes, and occasional notes from my writing desk. Unsubscribe anytime—no hard feelings.

Ready for what's next?

If you enjoyed Gin and Grudges the series doesn't end here. The next book in the series follows Camilla and Jameson with:

- brother's best friend

- outdoor 'play'

- slow burn

- An FMC that dreams of a life other than what she is 'supposed' to have

He's loved her forever. But he promised to let her go.

Pre-order Book 2 now
Be there from the very first page.
PRE-ORDER BOOK 2 in the Blackwood Valley series: https://store.laurenparkerrhodes.com/b/jP2 Mt
Pre-ordering helps support this series and ensures you don't miss the moment it goes live.

If this story stayed with you, I'd love to keep you close.
— Lauren Parker Rhodes

Thank you so much for reading! I truly hope you enjoyed Kade and Temperance's story and I can't wait to share more of Blackwood Valley with you. This book wouldn't have been possible without my gorgeous readers, my editor, critique partners, beta readers, and, of course, my amazing family.

About the Author

Escaping to fantasy worlds is a specialty of Lauren's, either creating her own or reading other people's – providing there's a strong romance, Lauren is all in. Living in semi-rural Australia with her husband and two little wildlings, Lauren tries to teach her children of the wonders of nature. About the impact of all our tiny decisions and that, sometimes, it only takes one person to make a difference. When she's not living vicariously through her characters, or kid-wrangling, Lauren can be found at her second home, the coast; feeding her coffee and chocolate addiction; or trying to fit in a yoga class...even though Archie the labrador would much prefer a walk.

Instagram: @laurenparkerrhodes
www.laurenparkerrhodes.com

www.ingramcontent.com/pod-product-compliance
Lightning Source LLC
Chambersburg PA
CBHW011926050726
47591CB00009B/2365